...naos

Cat in the Candlelight

Illustrations by Ann Baum

Siamese in the Sun

Illustrations by Ann Baum

LUCY DANIELS

Hodder
Children's
Books

A division of Hachette Children's Books

This bind-up edition published in 2013 by Hodder Children's Books

Thanks to C.J. Hall, B.Vet.Med., M.R.C.V.S. for reviewing the veterinary
information contained in *Cat in the Candlelight*

Cat in the Candlelight
Special thanks to Andrea Abbott

Text copyright © 2002 Working Partners Limited
Illustrations copyright © 2002 Ann Baum
First published as a single volume in Great Britain in 2002
by Hodder Children's Books

Siamese in the Sun
For Mary Tapissier, who has been a good friend to Animal Ark; her advice and
ideas have always been very much appreciated.
Special thanks to Ingrid Maitland

Text copyright © 2004 Working Partners Limited
Illustrations copyright © 2004 Ann Baum
First published as a single volume in Great Britain in 2004
by Hodder Children's Books

Animal Ark is a trademark of Working Partners Limited
Created by Working Partners Limited, London, WC1X 9HH
Original series created by Ben M. Baglio

A Catalogue record for this book is available from the British Library

ISBN 978 1 444 91465 8

Typeset in Baskerville Book by Avon DataSet Ltd, Bidford-on-Avon

Printed and bound in Great Britain by Clays Ltd, St Ives plc, Bungay, Suffolk

The paper and board used in this paperback by Hodder Children's Books
are natural recyclable products made from wood grown in sustainable
forests. The manufacturing processes conform to the environmental
regulations of the country of origin.

Hodder Children's Books
a division of Hachette Children's Books
338 Euston Road, London NW1 3BH
An Hachette UK company

www.hodderchildrens.co.uk

Cat
in the
Candlelight

ANIMAL
ARK
VETERINARY
SURGERY

One

A sudden strong gust of wind almost knocked Mandy Hope off her bicycle. 'Yikes!' she exclaimed, feeling the bike wobble beneath her. She steadied herself and carried on down the lane.

The wind blew an icy sheet of rain into her face. For a moment Mandy was blinded. She blinked, then wiped her eyes with her arm. 'I'll be soaked by the time I get home,' she muttered to herself. 'Trust it to start raining like this just in time for the Christmas holidays!'

She swerved to avoid a big puddle, then

pedalled on as fast as she could. Before long, she could see the Animal Ark sign at the end of the lane. It stood out against the grey cloudy sky and swayed back and forth in the wind, its hinges creaking loudly. Relieved, Mandy whizzed beneath it and sped up the driveway to the old stone cottage where she lived.

Her father was standing in the doorway of the modern veterinary surgery that was attached to the back of the cottage. Mandy's parents were vets and they ran Animal Ark, in the Yorkshire village of Welford.

'Is that a drowned rat coming to be revived?' Adam Hope's cheerful voice called out, as Mandy jumped off her bike outside the shed in the back garden.

'Almost drowned, Dad,' Mandy called back. She wheeled her bike into the shed, shut the door, then ran across the soggy lawn towards the surgery. 'And the only thing that can revive me is a big mug of hot chocolate!'

'You're in luck there – your mum's just made some,' smiled Adam Hope as they went inside. 'Sorry you had to battle the elements to get home, love,' he continued, closing the door behind them. 'I'd have picked you up from school if we hadn't been so busy all morning.'

'That's OK, Dad,' Mandy said. She dumped her bag on the floor then took off her dripping raincoat and hung it on the coat-stand next to the door. 'And anyway, it only started raining when I was about halfway home.' Mandy's school was in the town of Walton, about two miles away.

Animal Ark's receptionist, Jean Knox, looked up from her computer. 'Let's hope it stops raining as quickly as it started,' she said. 'My grandchildren are coming to stay tomorrow. They'll be here until after Christmas, and the last thing I need is for them to be cooped up indoors.'

Adam Hope nodded and grinned sympathetically.

'Still, with any luck, all this wind will blow the rain away,' Jean went on, trying to sound positive.

'No chance of that, I'm afraid,' said Emily Hope, coming into the reception. She went over to Mandy and hugged her. 'Lucky it was the last day of term and you came out early, love. There's just been a warning on the radio about strong gales later on. And the weatherman said we're in for really severe conditions for at least the next few days.'

'Oh, no!' Mandy exclaimed, her voice filled with frustration. 'James and I were going to do some cross-country cycling in the woods this week.'

James Hunter was Mandy's best friend. He lived on the other side of Welford village.

'But I guess we can always wait until after Christmas,' Mandy continued. 'And in the meantime, I'll have loads of time to help out around here.'

Mandy had her regular duties at Animal Ark, like feeding sick and recovering animals in the residential unit and cleaning out their cages. But she was always ready to help out in other ways during her spare time.

'Well, if today's anything to go by, you'll be rushed off your feet,' said Adam Hope, checking the big blue appointment book on the desk.

'That's fine by me,' Mandy smiled.

'It's lucky for us that you're going to be around,' said Emily Hope. 'We've already admitted three animals to the residential unit today and they'll need plenty of attention.'

'I'll go and see to them as soon as I've changed out of these wet clothes,' Mandy said, looking down at her navy blue school trousers which clung to her legs. She turned to go into the cottage.

'Don't forget your hot chocolate,' Mr Hope called out after her. 'It's on the counter.'

'And there's a slice of pizza in the oven for your lunch,' added Emily Hope.

Mandy went into the kitchen, gulped down her hot chocolate, then, taking the pizza with her, ran upstairs to change.

Five minutes later, she returned to the reception room where a woman and her young daughter were waiting. On the bench between them was a travelling basket. Mandy remembered them from a previous visit when they'd brought in a cat. 'Hello, Mrs Wilson,' she said to the woman. Then, peering into the basket she asked the girl, 'Who have you got in here today, Beth?'

'Stardust,' said the child. 'She's not very well.'

Inside the basket was a silver-grey chinchilla. The little animal sneezed once then stared out at Mandy.

'Hello, pretty one,' Mandy said. Despite the warmth in the room, Stardust was shivering. 'You don't look very happy,' Mandy added.

'She hasn't eaten all day,' said Beth in a serious voice. 'And she sneezes like that a lot.' She pushed her fingers through the cage and stroked

the chinchilla's soft fur. 'But don't worry, Stardust, the vets will make you better.' She looked up anxiously at Mandy. 'They will, won't they?'

Mandy smiled at her. 'Of course,' she said, straightening up as her mum came out of the treatment room.

'You can bring Stardust in now,' said Emily Hope to Mrs Wilson. 'Oh, and Mandy, will you give me a hand please? Simon's helping Dad with an injured puppy.'

Simon was the practice nurse. He had been at

Animal Ark for about three years.

'What happened to the puppy?' asked Mandy, following her mum into the treatment room.

'He managed to get his head stuck in a gate,' Mrs Hope told her. 'It's taken his owners almost an hour to get him out so he's pretty bruised and upset.'

Mandy winced, thinking how the puppy must have struggled to free himself.

In the treatment room, Mandy took Stardust out of her basket and put her on the table so that Mrs Hope could examine her. The chinchilla sneezed again several times, then lay so listlessly that Mandy didn't even need to hold her still.

'She's completely exhausted,' said Mrs Hope. She listened to Stardust's chest through her stethoscope. 'She's battling to breathe,' she remarked. 'And this nasal discharge isn't a good sign.' She listened a little longer, then removed the stethoscope and said to Mrs Wilson, 'Stardust's got a respiratory disease. I'll give her an antibiotic to clear up the infection, then we'll try to ease her breathing with some steam.' She took a small bottle of medication out of a cupboard. Mandy handed her a syringe and Mrs Hope filled it with the antibiotic then gently injected it into the chinchilla.

'Good girl,' Mrs Hope soothed, massaging the chinchilla's skin where the needle had gone in. Then she crouched down in front of Beth. 'Stardust needs to stay in hospital for a few days,' she explained. 'It's just so that we can keep an eye on her. But don't worry. She'll soon be back to her old self again.'

When Mrs Wilson and Beth had left, Mandy took Stardust into the residential unit and settled her into a clean cage. Then she turned her attention to the other animals that had been admitted that day.

There was a young greyhound in an enclosure against the wall. He'd broken a bone in one front leg, and looked rather sorry for himself with his bulky white plaster cast. In another cage on an opposite shelf was a drowsy cat which was recovering from an operation to remove an infected tooth. The third patient was a guinea-pig that had gone off its food.

Mandy gave them all fresh water and removed the soiled newspaper from the greyhound's cage. The dog was pleased to see her and wagged his tail rapidly while Mandy stroked him. She smiled when he crossed his front legs in the way she'd seen other dogs of the breed doing so often. 'Even with that cast, you still look elegant,' she laughed.

She looked in on Stardust once more then went back to the reception room where Jean was bustling about, preparing to go home.

The grey-haired woman turned to Mandy. 'The weather must be really bad,' she said. 'My daughter has just rung to say she isn't going to bring the children over after all. It's a pity, but I suppose it's better that they stay where they are.'

Above the howling of the wind outside, there came the sound of an engine revving up.

'Oh, good! Simon's managed to start his van at last,' said Jean, picking up her umbrella and opening the door. 'He's giving me a lift home.' She glanced uneasily at the battered old vehicle in the car park outside. 'I just hope it keeps going. I don't fancy walking back in this weather.'

'I'm sure it'll be fine,' Mandy reassured her. 'Simon usually has to give the engine a bit of extra encouragement to start in cold weather. But once it gets going, it goes like a bomb!'

'As long as it doesn't explode like one,' chuckled Jean, going outside.

Mandy stood at the door and waved as the old

vehicle rattled down the driveway. When it was out of sight, she went back to the residential unit where her parents were giving the patients their last treatment of the day.

While Mr Hope gave the cat its medication, Mandy helped her mother with Stardust. They put a bowl of steaming water next to the cage then draped a thick towel over both bowl and cage so that Stardust could breathe in the steam.

Mrs Hope added a few drops of eucalyptus oil to the water. 'That should help to clear her airways,' she said. She glanced out of the window. The wind battered the trees in the garden while the rain poured down. 'Of course, this cold wet weather won't help very much,' she warned.

When all the animals had been seen to, the Hopes went into the cottage to prepare supper. They were just sitting down to eat when there was a loud grating noise above them.

'Oh no,' said Adam Hope. 'It sounds like we've lost that loose tile I've been meaning to fix.'

'Does that mean we'll get a leak?' asked Mrs Hope anxiously.

'Could do,' said Mr Hope glumly. 'The weather's too bad to go up on the roof at the moment. I'll have to check on it in the morning.'

After supper they went into the living room to watch the news. The top story was the bad weather that was sweeping across most of Yorkshire. There were already several reports of serious damage, with Walton being one of the worst-affected places so far. The Hopes watched closely as the screen showed wind-ravaged properties in and around the town.

'Hey!' Mandy exclaimed as a familiar building came on to the screen. 'That's my school!' A large tree had blown down, crashing into the building and smashing several windows. 'I'm sure those are the windows in the science laboratory,' she said. But before she had a chance to look more closely, the newscaster moved on to another story.

'I guess you'll find out all about it when you go back after Christmas,' said Mr Hope, getting up to put another log on the fire.

'I wonder if James saw it?' Mandy pondered.

'Phone him and find out,' suggested Mrs Hope.

Mandy went into the hall and dialled the Hunters' number.

'Did you see the news?' Mandy asked James as he answered the phone.

'No,' replied James. 'I've been in the loft, sorting out our Christmas decorations.'

Mandy told him what she'd just seen.

'Just as well it wasn't the classrooms,' James joked, 'or we'd have been in for a draughty time when school starts again!'

'I'm sure the storm will have cleared up before then,' Mandy said.

'It had better clear up before Christmas,' remarked James firmly. 'We haven't even got our tree yet, and Dad doesn't want to bring one back on the roof of the car in case the wind blows it off.'

'We haven't got one either,' Mandy said. As she spoke, the lamp on the table next to her dimmed slightly, then brightened up again. 'It looks like the wind's having a fine old time battering the electricity lines,' she observed. 'Our lights are flickering here.'

'Ours too,' said James. 'I guess I'd better not check the bulbs in our fairy lights tonight. I won't be able to tell if they're flashing properly or not!'

'I was going to check ours too—' Mandy began, but before she could finish her sentence, she was plunged into darkness . . .

Two

'Hey! We've had a power cut!' Mandy exclaimed.

'Us too,' answered James. 'I'd better help Mum and Dad find some candles.'

'Bye, James,' Mandy said. She hung up, then felt her way along the wall of the hall back to the living room. The soft orange glow of the fire spread a shadowy light around the room. Mandy could see her dad hunting about in the drawers beneath the TV unit. 'I'm sure there's a torch in here somewhere,' he said.

'I'll get some candles from the kitchen,' Mandy offered.

It was pitch black in there. Mandy couldn't see a thing in front of her. 'Ouch!' she muttered, knocking her funny bone against the corner of the dresser. She rubbed her elbow which tingled uncomfortably. *Why do they call it a funny bone when it isn't at all funny to bump it?* she wondered.

She groped around inside the dresser cupboard until she found a packet of candles and an old lantern. 'This'll do,' she said.

There was a box of matches on the dresser. Mandy struck one, then lit a candle and put it inside the lantern. The faint flickering light cast long-fingered shadows around the room.

'Here comes Florence Nightingale,' laughed Adam Hope when Mandy returned to the living room. He picked up some iron tongs and prodded the fire. There was a loud crackling and popping as orange sparks flew up the chimney.

'Isn't this cosy?' said Mr Hope, putting down the tongs and settling back into his chair.

'Mmm. But I hope it doesn't go on too long,' said his wife.

'I'm sure it won't,' Mr Hope said cheerfully. 'You'll probably find a tree has fallen on to some power lines and a repair team is already on its way.'

'I hope you're right,' said Mrs Hope. 'I was planning to catch up on some paperwork tonight. And I don't feel like doing it by candlelight.'

'Let's play cards by candlelight instead,' suggested Adam Hope.

'And toast some marshmallows on the fire,' Mandy added.

'Excellent idea!' grinned her dad.

Mandy fetched a bag of coconut-coated marshmallows and some long forks from the kitchen. Back in the living room, the three of them speared the marshmallows on to the ends of the forks then held them over the flames.

'Smells delicious!' declared Adam Hope, licking his lips as the aroma of toasted coconut wafted out from the fire. 'I'm almost glad we've got no electricity. We wouldn't have done this otherwise.'

They played cards and toasted marshmallows for the rest of the evening, all the while expecting the lights to come back on. But by ten-thirty, there was still no power.

Mrs Hope yawned and stood up. 'Time for bed, I think.'

'Yes. It's been a long day,' said Adam Hope,

standing up to stretch. He put the wrought-iron guard in front of the fire. 'And there's not much point sitting around waiting for the lights to come back on.'

They went upstairs, with Mandy carrying the lantern to light their way. She thought about the animals in the residential unit. The darkness wouldn't really bother them. But it was a good thing that Animal Ark had gas heating – especially since the chinchilla needed to be kept warm.

'Don't forget to blow out the candle before you go to sleep, Mandy,' said Mrs Hope at the top of the stairs.

'And make sure your bedside light is switched off, otherwise you'll be dazzled in the night if the electricity comes back on,' warned her dad.

But the power didn't come on during the night. And when Mandy woke early in the morning, the wind was still raging, and the rain was pelting hard against the windows.

She climbed out of bed and drew back the curtains. 'Look at that!' she exclaimed, startled at the sight that met her. 'What a mess!' Enormous puddles covered most of the garden, and fallen branches lay strewn all around. Mandy washed and dressed and was on her way downstairs when the phone rang.

She heard her dad answering it. 'I'll be there as soon as I can,' he said.

'What's happened, Dad?' Mandy asked, meeting him at the foot of the stairs.

'A cow's been badly hurt at Garland Farm,' said Adam Hope.

They went into the kitchen where Mrs Hope was putting a pot of water on the Aga range which the family used in winter. 'Just as well we've got this old stove,' she said. 'But all the same, the tea's going to take a bit longer than usual, I'm afraid.'

'I'll just have some orange juice for now,' said Adam Hope, pouring himself a glass from a jug on the table. 'But I expect I'll need a hot drink when I get back from Garland's.'

'How did the cow get hurt?' Mandy asked him.

'A barn collapsed and some heavy timbers fell on the poor creature,' her dad explained.

'Doesn't sound too good,' said Emily Hope, shaking her head sympathetically. 'Was it just one animal that was injured?'

'It seems to be,' said Mr Hope, gulping down the juice then picking up the car keys from the dresser. 'I'll just fetch my bag from the surgery, then I'll be on my way.'

'Be careful,' Emily Hope told him. 'That farm's really low-lying. There might be some flooding in that area.'

'I'll be all right in the Land-rover,' answered Mr Hope, taking a heavy waterproof jacket from a peg behind the door. 'I shouldn't be too long.'

Minutes later he was back in the kitchen, looking rather frustrated and very wet.

'What's the matter?' Mandy asked, through a mouthful of muesli.

'I can't get out of the garage,' Mr Hope explained. 'There's a massive branch lying just in front of it. I can't budge it on my own so I need some help to clear it out of the way.'

Mandy and Mrs Hope pulled on their wellington boots and raincoats and followed him outside. The wind whipped around them, tugging at their coats and driving stinging bursts of rain into their faces.

'It's much worse out here than I thought,' Mandy shouted above the roaring gale. She sloshed through puddles that were already ankle deep in places. Even the driveway was covered in water. 'I wonder what it's like in the lane?' she asked.

'Probably a lot like it is here,' said Mr Hope. 'But I'll find out – just as soon as I can get past this.' He kicked at the enormous branch that blocked the garage door.

'It's more a tree trunk than a branch,' said Mrs Hope. She wiped a wet strand of hair out of her eyes then looked up at a nearby oak tree. 'That's where it came from,' she said, pointing to a ragged gash half-way up the trunk. 'We're lucky it didn't fall on the roof.'

'Just shows how strong this gale is if it can break something this big,' said Mr Hope. He bent down and slid his hands under one end of the log. 'You two take the other end.'

With much heaving and straining, they finally managed to shift the heavy branch to one side. Mr Hope drove away, the wheels of the Land-rover shooting huge sprays of water to either side.

Mrs Hope and Mandy watched him go before paddling round to the surgery. 'Let's check on the animals and brace ourselves for whatever else the day has in store for us!' remarked Mrs Hope.

'You mean more rain?' Mandy frowned, looking up at the heavy skies.

'It certainly looks like it,' said her mother.

They pulled off their wellies and went inside. Already, the phone was ringing again.

Mandy answered it. It was Mrs Ponsonby. 'I don't want to take Pandora and Toby out in such atrocious conditions,' she boomed. Pandora was a spoilt Pekinese and Toby was a mongrel puppy. 'So they won't be in for their check-up today. I'll make another appointment when this ghastly rain and wind have stopped.'

Mrs Ponsonby wasn't the only person to cancel her appointment. Minutes later, another pet owner rang up to say she'd rather not come out in the bad weather.

Two more phone calls followed in quick succession. First, Jean Knox rang to say she couldn't get in because a mudslide had blocked her road. 'The council says they're so busy dealing with emergencies, they won't be able to clear it up until tomorrow,' she said, sounding flustered.

Then Simon called to say that his van wouldn't start. 'I think the engine must have got waterlogged when I was driving home last night,' he told Mandy.

'I'm amazed to hear you even made it home

after the way it was spluttering yesterday,' Mandy teased.

'There's nothing wrong with my van,' said Simon defensively. 'It just doesn't like water.'

'You mean it doesn't like *working*,' Mandy joked, before hanging up.

Mrs Hope studied the remaining appointments in the diary. 'You know, none of these cases is particularly urgent,' she said to Mandy, 'so I think we should cancel them all. I'm sure most people won't relish coming out today.'

They contacted the pet owners, who were very happy to bring their animals in a day or two later. Then Emily Hope rang the electricity department to find out when they could expect the power to come back on. 'Not for several more days!' she echoed with astonishment upon hearing the reply.

She hung up, shaking her head. 'Apparently the gale brought down a pylon and some major power lines,' she explained to Mandy. 'And it's a huge job to sort it all out. So we're stuck with candles and fires for the time being.'

Mandy shrugged. 'I'm getting quite used to not switching on the lights,' she said, following her mum into the residential unit.

The greyhound must have heard them before they came in because he was waiting at the gate to his cage, his slim body trembling with excitement.

'Hello, Marco,' said Mrs Hope, opening the gate and checking his leg. 'I think you can go home today – if your owner can make it here to fetch you!'

'And how are you today, Stardust?' Mandy asked, going over to the chinchilla.

Stardust looked just as miserable as before. She hadn't touched her food and was still having trouble breathing. She wheezed noisily, in short, shallow breaths. 'I don't think *you're* ready to go home,' Mandy said.

Mrs Hope joined Mandy next to the cage. 'I'll give her another injection in a minute. In the meantime, you can give her the steam and eucalyptus treatment again. I'll go and switch the kettle on to boil some . . .' She stopped. 'Oh no! I forgot,' she grumbled. 'No electricity!'

'I'll fetch some hot water from the kitchen,' Mandy offered. 'It's lucky you put that pan on the Aga at breakfast time.' She fetched the water and set up Stardust's steam treatment.

Mrs Hope was examining the cat and the guinea-pig. When she'd seen to them, she came over to Mandy. 'They're much better,' she said. 'I'd like them to go home, like Marco. We'll ring their owners to let them know.'

But only the cat's owner said he'd come round immediately. Marco and the guinea-pig's owners were reluctant to come out just then. They asked if they could wait until later in the day to see if the weather improved.

'Never mind,' Mandy said, stroking the guinea-pig who was now hungrily munching up her food. 'We'll take good care of you here.'

'Still, I'm sure they'll be happier in their own surroundings,' said Mrs Hope. 'Perhaps Dad will be able to take them home when he comes back.'

'After he's had his hot drink,' Mandy reminded her mum with a smile.

The cat's owner arrived within twenty minutes. 'Just as well I drive a jeep,' he said. 'Most of the roads are several centimetres under water. If it carries on raining like this, the river might burst its banks, and then we could be in for some serious flooding.' He draped a plastic sheet over the cat's basket then dashed outside and drove away, churning up a wake on the driveway behind him.

By the time Adam Hope came home later that morning, the garden was even more waterlogged. The huge puddles on the lawn were growing by the minute. A lot of them had even joined up to form bigger ones. Mandy watched the Land-rover splashing through the water as it came up the drive. *It looks as though Dad's driving through a river*, she thought to herself.

She pulled on her wellies again and waded out to meet him. 'Is the cow all right?' she asked, entering the garage.

'She will be,' Mr Hope replied, climbing out of the Land-rover. 'She's badly cut and bruised, so she's in a lot of pain. But luckily nothing was broken. I said I'd check on her again tomorrow.' He looked out at the teeming rain. 'I just hope I'll be able to make it there,' he said grimly. 'It's pretty heavy going right now and it's worsening by the minute.'

Mandy took a deep breath. 'Would you mind risking one more trip today?' she asked her dad.

Mr Hope looked at her aghast. 'You mean go out in this weather again?'

'Uh-huh,' Mandy nodded. 'You see we need

to take Marco and the guinea-pig home,' she explained. 'Their owners are worried about coming out.'

'And what about poor me having to risk life and limb again?' grinned Mr Hope.

'But you've got a Land-rover, and it won't take long, Dad,' Mandy said. 'They live quite close to each other. And I'll help you.'

Adam Hope jangled his keys. 'Well, if we're to make it back home again before the lane's completely flooded, we'd better get a move on.'

Mandy ran back to the residential unit. She put the guinea-pig in a basket then took Marco out of his cage. 'Sorry, Stardust,' she said, glancing across to the chinchilla's cage. 'It won't be long before you can go home too.'

Mr Hope came in and picked up the guinea-pig's basket. 'Ready?' he asked Mandy.

Mandy nodded. She tucked Marco inside her jacket to keep him dry, then followed her father back out to the garage.

'The animals went in two-by-two,' Mr Hope recited with a grin as he slid the guinea-pig's basket on to the back seat of the Land-rover.

'But not as *odd* pairs of animals, Dad,' laughed

Mandy. She climbed into the passenger seat then opened her jacket. Marco's long slender nose peeped out. He craned his arched neck and stared quizzically out of the window.

'Ready to set sail, Marco?' Mandy chuckled as Mr Hope reversed out of the garage then turned the Land-rover and set off for the village. As they passed under the Animal Ark sign, Mandy saw at once why her dad was worried about the lane. It was already several inches under water.

'I'm not sure this is wise,' said Mr Hope, steering carefully through the flood. But he pressed on and soon they were on higher ground, heading for the housing estate on the other side of the village.

They delivered the animals to their grateful owners then turned for home. It was lunchtime as they came to the Fox and Goose, the pub in the centre of Welford. Usually people would be arriving for a meal now. But, today, there wasn't anybody about. And, even worse, the Christmas lights which festooned the low stone building no longer lent the place a cheerful air. Instead, they clung damply to the eaves, their bulbs extinguished and water dripping constantly from them.

'It's so gloomy!' Mandy groaned.

The tall Christmas tree in front of the pub was surrounded by an enormous puddle. Someone had tied a thick rope to the trunk of the tree and secured it to a post nearby.

'I suppose that's to stop it being blown down or washed away,' said Mr Hope.

'The poor thing looks almost sad,' Mandy commented. The tree's branches, heavy with water, sagged limply towards the ground, twitching in the wind. And on the top the silver star hung down, crumpled and battered out of shape.

'It's not at all like Christmas,' Mandy murmured. 'If only this horrid weather would clear up.'

'Not much chance of that for a day or two,' said her dad, turning into the lane. The drains on both sides of the narrow road had become blocked and were spewing rubbish and more water out into the lane. 'But just think how terrific it will be when it eventually *does* stop raining and all of this clears up,' Mr Hope added, gesturing ahead of him.

The Land-rover bumped along, its wheels churning up the puddles into a muddy brown froth. At last, they came to Animal Ark.

'Home sweet home,' Mandy grinned. But as

they started up the driveway, she gasped. The cottage was almost completely surrounded by water. 'It's like an island!' she said.

Mr Hope drove into the garage. Water was beginning to seep in under the door so that Mandy and her dad stepped down from the Land-rover into a pool on the floor.

Mr Hope looked troubled. 'This is getting serious,' he said. 'The river must have burst its banks, and flooded all the way up here. We're going to have to stop the water from coming in.' He looked around the garage. A row of bulky bags stood against the back wall. 'Those sacks of compost might do the trick.'

'You mean, use them like sandbags?' Mandy asked.

'Uh-huh,' nodded her dad. 'We'll stack them up outside the door.' Working fast, they lined the bags up in front of the garage door. Every time she stooped to wedge another bag into place, Mandy felt raindrops seeping down her neck.

'Not quite as good as sand,' said Mr Hope. 'But it's all we have.'

By the time they had finished, they were both drenched. They ran through the teeming rain to the front porch where Mrs Hope was waiting for them. 'You're just in the nick of time,' she told them as they went indoors. 'I've heard on the radio that the river has burst its banks upstream. The weather office has put out a severe flood warning for Welford.'

'We're going to be marooned,' said Mandy.

'Probably,' said Mrs Hope. 'Let's just hope that the house doesn't get flooded.'

Mr Hope nodded gravely. Then a smile spread across his face. 'At least we're in an ark,' he said. His joke lightened the gloomy atmosphere.

'Let's hope it's a waterproof ark,' smiled Mrs Hope.

'Not if Dad's roof repairs are anything to go by,' Mandy said, looking up to the ceiling where a damp patch had formed.

Her father grimaced. 'It never rains but it pours,' he said with a sigh. He thought for a second. 'I guess I'd better have a go at fixing that now before it develops into a major problem.'

'Good idea, Noah,' chuckled Mrs Hope. 'And while you're up there, Mandy and I will see to Stardust again.'

Alone in the residential unit, the chinchilla looked more dejected than ever. But just when Mandy was wondering if the little animal was ever going to get better, Stardust hopped over to her food bowl and began nibbling on one of the pellets.

'Good girl,' Mandy said encouragingly. She turned to her mum. 'Shouldn't we take her into the cottage with us? She's very lonely in here.'

Mrs Hope smiled at Mandy and shook her head in amusement. 'Mandy Hope. The vet-to-be with a heart of gold!'

'We can keep her in the living room in her cage so we don't have to keep coming in here to check on her,' Mandy said persuasively.

Emily Hope shrugged her shoulders. 'Well, I don't see the harm in it. And you're right. Since she's our only patient, we might as well have her in the cottage.'

They put Stardust in a portable cage and carried her into the living room. The chinchilla looked around her new surroundings with interest then began nibbling her food again.

* * *

After lunch, James phoned up. 'Are you floating yet?' he asked Mandy.

'Nearly,' she replied, gazing out of the hall window at the rising flood water. And then she saw something else – something bright red bobbing about outside.

'Hey! What's that?' she said, standing up and leaning towards the window for a better look.

'What's what?' came James's confused voice.

'It's a little boat!' Mandy exclaimed.

'A toy one?' asked James.

'No. It's real. And hang on, there's another . . . and another! Just a minute, James.' She dropped the receiver on to the table and ran over to the door.

Behind her, James's puzzled voice called down the line, 'Mandy! What's going on? Where are you?'

Mandy opened the front door. An amazing sight greeted her. Animal Ark was besieged by a flotilla of small rowing boats! Unmanned, they bobbed about on the water, their oars stowed neatly in their shafts.

'Mandy!' called out James again. 'What's happened?'

Mandy turned and picked up the phone. 'You won't believe this, James,' she said. 'But Animal Ark has just become a harbour!'

Three

'James reckons they're from that boat-hire company on the river,' Mandy told her mum and dad after ringing off from James and calling them to see the boats.

'That makes sense,' agreed Mrs Hope. 'The gale must have made them break their moorings. Then they floated down here when the river flooded.'

'We'd better let the hire company know where they are,' said Mr Hope, flipping through the telephone directory to find the number.

The owner, Andrew Bond, was hugely relieved to find out where his boats were. He said he'd arrange to have them collected as soon as the floods subsided.

'That might not be for days,' Mandy said to her mum and dad, staring out at the driving rain. 'What if they float off somewhere else in the meantime?'

'I don't think that'll happen,' said Mr Hope. 'They're already clustering together at the side of the garage. It looks like the current comes to a stop there so it's a sort of natural mooring.'

Except for one boat which was firmly jammed against the front steps, all the boats gradually converged next to the garage. Drifting along on the tide, they edged closer together, bumping and jostling one another, their bright colours looking almost festive on the grey water. *Just as well I've finished all my shopping*, Mandy thought. With only five days to go before Christmas, and the flood water rising, she might not have had another chance to do it.

She spent the rest of the afternoon half-heartedly sorting through decorations and hanging tinsel around the fireplace. There was an artificial Christmas tree in the loft and Mandy hauled it down to the living room. 'Not as nice as a real one but I suppose it's better than nothing,' she said to her parents. 'Of course, some fairy lights would help!' she sighed, fed up that the power was still off.

From her cage nearby, Stardust stared out at the tree.

'Do you want to have a closer look?' Mandy said to the chinchilla. She gently lifted her out of the cage and carried her over to the tree.

Stardust sniffed at the lower branches, but she quickly lost interest in the artificial leaves and hopped away to investigate a plant. She started to nibble at a leaf then stopped and twitched her nose before making a bee-line for a bowl of hazelnuts on the hearth.

'Hey! Those are mine!' said Adam Hope, scooping up the dish just as Stardust dipped her head into it.

The chinchilla sat back, a look of disappointment on her fluffy face.

'Don't be mean, Dad,' laughed Mandy. 'It's Christmas, remember? The season of goodwill. You should be sharing.'

Mr Hope gave her a lopsided grin. 'I'll remember that the next time I see you tucking into something delicious!' He reached down and gave Stardust a hazelnut. The chinchilla quickly munched it up then looked up at him, hoping for another.

'She's so much better,' said Mrs Hope. 'It's a shame we're cut off like this – she could have gone home this afternoon.'

Mandy picked up Stardust and cuddled her velvety soft body. 'I'm not sorry you're stuck with us,' she whispered. 'You're really sweet and it will be fun to have you around for a few more days.'

'Just as well she's our only patient,' said Mr Hope, putting the nuts on the mantelpiece, well out of Stardust's reach. 'Otherwise you'd have had me sharing my meals with all and sundry!'

'No danger of that for a day or two,' said Mrs Hope. 'I can't imagine anyone even trying to bring an animal to us now.'

'But what if there's an emergency?' Mandy asked, suddenly feeling worried. She carried Stardust back to her cage and put her inside.

'Let's not worry about things that haven't happened,' said Mr Hope.

'But what *would* you do if an animal fell seriously ill?' Mandy persisted, flopping down on the sofa.

Mr Hope looked thoughtful for a moment. He smoothed his beard with one hand then said, 'We'd make a plan, but don't ask me now what it would be. We'll just have to cross that bridge when – and if – the time comes.'

Mandy's worst fears were realised the very next day when the phone rang during breakfast.

Emily Hope went into the hall then came back a minute later. 'It's Walter Pickard,' she said. 'He's worried about Scraps. She's gone off her food.'

Walter Pickard was a retired butcher who lived in a cottage behind the Fox and Goose. He had three cats, Scraps and Missie, who were both ginger and rather old, and Tom, a black and white tomcat.

'That's unusual for Scraps,' Mandy commented. 'She normally eats anything.'

'Are there any other symptoms?' asked Mr Hope.

'Walter said she's very lethargic and that she's been soiling her basket lately,' said Emily Hope. 'It doesn't sound too good. I explained to Walter that we're cut off, but said we'd try to arrange something.' She looked anxiously out of the kitchen window at the flood water. 'But what?'

'I'll contact Steve Wimberley from the practice in Walton and see if he can get through to him,' said Adam Hope. 'I was going to ask if he could see to the Garland's cow anyway, seeing as I can't get to the farm now.'

Mr Hope contacted the Walton vet who said he could make it to Garland Farm because it was on the other side of the river from Welford. But the road into the village was completely underwater so he wouldn't be able to get to Walter.

'That just means we have to come up with another plan, Dad,' Mandy said in a matter-of-fact voice. Scraps simply *had* to get the treatment she needed. Mandy never gave up on a sick animal, no matter how difficult the circumstances were. 'Even if we have to *walk* there!' she added earnestly.

'It's more likely we'll have to *swim*,' her dad pointed out, going over to the window. 'That water out there's not just knee-deep any more.'

'There's got to be a way of getting through,' said Mandy, her mind searching for an idea. And then it came to her. 'The boats!' she exclaimed. 'That's the answer. We can *row* to Walter's!'

Mr Hope clicked his fingers. 'Good thinking, Mandy,' he declared. 'And luckily there's one still wedged up against the front steps. We shouldn't even have to get our feet wet!'

They rang the hire company to ask if they could borrow the boat. The owner was very happy to oblige. 'Glad to be of some service in a crisis,' he said.

Within minutes, Mandy and her dad were ready to go. They went out to the porch and Mr Hope reached for the boat that was still wedged against the steps. 'I'll hold it steady while you get in,' he told Mandy.

Gingerly, Mandy climbed into the boat. It wobbled violently and she had to grab the sides to stop herself from falling out. 'Phew!' she breathed, sitting down quickly.

Mr Hope handed her his bulky vet's bag then tried to get in with her. But before he had both feet in the boat, it began to drift away from the steps. 'Oops!' he exclaimed, swaying and teetering on his back foot as the gulf between the boat and the step widened.

But just when it seemed that Mr Hope would be pulled into the water, he heaved himself forward. 'Hold tight!' he cried, sitting down heavily next to Mandy. The little boat lurched under his weight and for a second Mandy thought it would capsize.

'Sorry about that, love,' said Mr Hope when the rocking subsided. 'But I had to make a leap for it!'

Mandy laughed. 'I wish I'd had a camera with me.'

'I'm glad you didn't,' smiled Mr Hope, picking up the oars and handing one to Mandy.

They struck out across the flooded garden then paddled under the Animal Ark sign. Mandy gasped when she saw that the lane had completely disappeared beneath the flood water. 'It's like a river!' she said.

'It *is* a river,' responded her dad. 'Now that the original one has burst its banks.'

The wind had eased but it was still strong enough to buffet the boat and whip up icy sprays of water which showered Mandy and her dad as they rowed along.

'The flood's washed down all sorts of things,' Mandy remarked, pointing to a tyre and a half-submerged plastic bucket that were being swept along in the swirling water ahead of them.

'Keep a look out for heavy things like uprooted trees,' said Mr Hope, deftly manoeuvring the boat past a thick branch that was rushing along next to them.

The swiftly flowing water helped to propel them onward so it wasn't long before they reached the crossroads in the centre of Welford. Like the previous day, there was little life in the village. And today, the Fox and Goose looked even more drab and uninviting. The car park was swamped, and muddy water lapped over the edge of the front porch.

Mandy and Adam Hope pulled on their oars, navigating the boat down the side of the pub to Walter's little cottage. They dragged the boat on to the top step then knocked on the battered front door.

'Thank goodness you managed to find a way to get here,' said Walter when he opened the door and saw the boat. He led them into his tiny living-room. Scraps was lying very still on a cushion near the fire. A bowl of cat biscuits and pieces of chicken sat beside her. Scraps opened her eyes when Mr Hope bent down in front of her but closed them again immediately. Mandy realised with a sinking feeling that the sick cat didn't have the energy to keep them open.

Mr Hope gently examined Scraps. He listened to her heart and lungs then felt her belly before finally taking a urine sample. While Mr Hope tested the sample, Walter and Mandy looked on apprehensively, hoping for news that would mean Scraps would soon be well again.

But Mr Hope could offer little comfort. 'I'm afraid things aren't looking too good for Scraps,' he said softly. 'I'm pretty certain her kidneys are failing. It's a common disease in ageing cats,' he told Walter. He took a syringe out of his bag and filled it with some medication. 'I'll give her a vitamin B injection to help deal with the build-up of toxins, but the main thing now is to keep her as comfortable as possible. And try to get her to drink, Walter. If she doesn't, I'll have to put her on a drip.'

'Oh, she's drinking quite a bit of water,' said Walter, his voice a mixture of hope and anxiety. 'That's a good sign, isn't it?'

Mr Hope smiled sympathetically but said nothing. He carefully injected Scraps then put the used needle into a disposal bag. Closing his vet's bag, he said, 'With a little encouragement, Scraps may start eating again, but I'm afraid I can't promise a dramatic improvement. After all, she is in her twilight years now.' He put a hand on Walter's shoulder and said kindly, 'I'm sorry, Walter.'

The old man swallowed hard and turned away. He knelt down next to Scraps and stroked her lightly. 'Poor old girl,' he murmured, his gentle voice breaking with emotion.

Mandy felt a lump forming in her throat. The last time she'd seen Scraps, she'd been sneaking a biscuit off the table in Walter's kitchen. And now she was lying so still, not showing the slightest interest in food. Mandy crouched down and kissed the top of the old cat's head. 'I'll come and see you again soon, Scraps,' she said.

As Mandy and Mr Hope turned to go, Tom, the black and white cat, came into the room. He was an unfriendly animal who usually ignored Walter's visitors. But, today, Mandy thought he seemed different. He walked over to Scraps and sniffed her. Then he sat next to her and gently licked the sick cat's ears.

'It looks like he's trying to comfort Scraps,' Mandy said with surprise.

'Aye. He's been fussing about her since yesterday,' said Walter. 'I've never seen him doing anything like it.'

'He must know that Scraps is ill. It just shows how little we understand of cats,' said Mr Hope. He opened the front door and said to Walter, 'I'll check on Scraps again in the morning. But if you need me before then, I'll come round right away.'

'Thanks, Adam,' said Walter hoarsely. 'I know you're doing everything you can.'

Mandy and Mr Hope climbed back into the boat. In silence, they paddled round to the front of the pub. They were halfway across the flooded green when Mandy spotted James in a small rubber dinghy. He was on the opposite side of the green, paddling strongly towards them.

'I wonder what he's up to?' Mandy mused.

James rowed over to them, the dinghy bouncing lightly over the choppy water.

'I've been fetching supplies for some of our neighbours,' he said, pointing to a box of groceries in front of him. 'Luckily Mrs McFarlane still had

some bread and milk in stock.'

Mrs McFarlane ran the local post office. It was the only shop in the village so she sold all sorts of things, including groceries.

'We've been on an urgent mission too,' Mandy said. She told James about Scraps. 'She's really very ill,' she finished.

'Poor old cat,' said James. 'And poor Walter. He'll be broken-hearted if anything happens to Scraps.'

'Unfortunately that's all part of giving your

heart to an animal,' said Adam Hope. 'Pets give us lots of joy but sooner or later we're in for heartache with them. And even though we may be prepared for it to happen, it's always a big wrench when it does.'

That night, Mandy lay in bed thinking of Walter and Scraps. She wondered just how much longer the two old friends had together. She hoped that Scraps was feeling a little better after the injection, and that she'd been able to eat something, even if it was only a temporary improvement.

She sighed. Her dad was right. With the joy of owning a pet came the sadness of parting with it. And even though Walter had two other cats which he adored, it would still be very hard for him if Scraps didn't make it.

She was about to blow out the candle in the lantern when she became aware of an odd bumping sound. It was coming from downstairs.

Stardust? Mandy wondered at once, remembering another chinchilla called Peanut which had got loose in Animal Ark and taken up residence in the chimney. *Surely she hasn't escaped from her cage? I thought I closed it properly.*

She pulled on her dressing gown then picked up the lantern and went downstairs. The bumping continued rhythmically. *It's not coming from in here after all*, Mandy decided, going into the living room.

All the same, she thought it best to check on Stardust. She went over to the cage. The gate was firmly closed and Stardust was fast asleep, tightly curled into a fluffy grey ball.

Mandy was puzzled. *So what is making that noise?* she thought.

She listened again and decided that the noise was coming from outside, near the front door. *It's probably the rowing boat knocking against the porch. I'll have to stop it, otherwise it'll keep me awake all night*, she decided.

Her wellies were standing next to the door in the hall. She pulled them on, expecting to slosh about in the water on the steps as she tried to grab the boat. But when she opened the door and stepped out on to the porch, she saw that the boat was quite still, its prow lodged securely on the top step.

Perplexed, Mandy looked around. The strange noise was coming from somewhere to her right.

She lifted the lantern higher, trying to see what was there.

And then, in the soft glow given off by the candle, she noticed a rounded object bumping against the cottage wall. Intrigued, she leaned out over the edge of the porch to get a closer look.

'Oh! It's only an old barrel,' she said to herself, recognising the shape. 'Just more flotsam washed down by the floods.' The wooden tub was bobbing upright in the water with its top end open.

She reached out to push the barrel away from the house but, as her hand caught hold of it, she saw a small movement inside.

And then she heard a faint sound.

'There's something in there!' Mandy exclaimed.

Quickly she pulled the barrel towards her. As it came into the candlelight she saw a pair of bright eyes staring up at her.

'It's a cat!' Mandy cried.

Four

'Oh, you poor thing,' Mandy breathed, reaching into the barrel with her free hand. She grasped the loose skin at the back of the cat's neck. In one smooth movement, she hauled the sodden little creature out and held it securely against her waist.

The barrel bobbed and lurched before being caught up once more in the current.

'Just in time,' Mandy said, as it drifted into the watery darkness. Beneath her arm, the cat trembled and shivered. 'Is that because you're cold, or afraid, or both?' Mandy said softly, looking down at the soggy little creature. It was black and white with big, staring green eyes.

Quickly Mandy went inside. She put the lantern on the table in the hall and prised off her boots with one hand while holding the cat in the other. Then, picking up the lantern again, she went into the kitchen.

There she found a clean, dry towel which she wrapped around the cat. 'We'll go next to the Aga where it's nice and warm,' she said, pulling a chair over to the cooker. She sat down and, holding the cat in her lap, gently towelled it dry.

'There. That's better,' Mandy said, unwrapping the towel after a few minutes. The cat's fur no longer clung damply to its skin. 'Now what's a pretty girl like you doing out on those floods?'

The cat was still shivering uncontrollably. She sat hunched in Mandy's lap and stared rigidly at a point somewhere ahead of her.

'Perhaps you're hungry,' Mandy wondered. Carefully, she eased the cat off her lap and put her on to another chair. Then she poured some milk into a saucer and held it in front of the tense little animal.

But the frightened cat showed no interest in the milk.

'I guess you're too shocked to want anything,' Mandy said. 'I just hope you're not hurt or ill.' She looked at the kitchen clock. The luminous hands showed that it was nearly midnight. 'It's ages to go before morning,' she said. 'I wish Mum or Dad would wake up.'

Mandy picked up the cat again and cuddled her closely, trying to help her relax. 'You still feel so cold. And I really don't like the way you're trembling.'

The cat fixed her bright green eyes on Mandy's face and stared at her pitifully.

Mandy made up her mind in an instant. 'You can't wait till morning,' she said decisively. 'I'm going to wake Mum and Dad. They'll understand when they see what a state you're in.'

But as she opened the door, she nearly collided with her mother who was coming into the kitchen at that same moment.

'I thought I heard something down here,' said Emily Hope. Then she saw the cat in Mandy's arms. 'And who is this?'

'An unexpected visitor, you could say,' Mandy

said. She quickly explained how she'd found the cat.

'Poor little creature,' said Mrs Hope. 'She must have been terrified. I'd better have a good look at her.' She took the cat from Mandy and carried her over to the kitchen table. 'Can you put a towel on the table and light a few more candles for me, Mandy?' she asked.

Mandy found another dry towel and spread it out on to the table. Then she fetched the candles from the living room and arranged them around the kitchen. They lent the room a warm, almost cheerful air. Mandy thought that in different circumstances, it would have looked quite festive.

'Would you bring me the emergency bag please, Mandy?' asked Mrs Hope. 'Dad left it in the hall this morning when you came back from Walter's.'

Mandy fetched the bag and Mrs Hope began by checking the cat's temperature. 'Mmm. A little on the cold side, but that's hardly surprising,' Mrs Hope murmured. She took out a stethoscope and listened to the animal's heartbeat and breathing. 'That's all fine,' she said, before examining the cat for signs of injury. Finally, with the help of a small torch, she checked her eyes and ears. At last Mrs Hope looked across at Mandy and said, 'Well, apart from being cold and in shock, she's absolutely fine. All she needs is to be kept warm and quiet for a few days.'

'That's easy,' Mandy said, relieved that the cat's watery adventure had caused her no real harm. 'And I think she ought to stay with me for the rest of the night.'

'Just tonight,' agreed Mrs Hope, blowing out the candles. 'Then tomorrow we'll put her – and Stardust – in the residential unit. Otherwise the cottage will really start to resemble an ark, especially if we have any more animals arriving unexpectedly!'

Cradling the cat in her arms, Mandy carried her upstairs. Mrs Hope followed behind, lighting the way with the lantern.

'Let's give her a name,' Mandy suggested. 'Even if it's just a temporary one.' She was sure the cat's owners would soon be looking for her, and then they'd find out what her real name was. But in the meantime, it would be nice to call her something.

'Any suggestions?' asked Mrs Hope, waiting with the lantern so that Mandy could see her way across to her bed.

Mandy studied the cat for a second. The candlelight danced against the little animal's black and white coat, highlighting now and again her white chest and her bright green eyes. The hazy, leaping glow triggered Mandy's imagination. 'What about Flicker?' she said.

'That suits her perfectly,' agreed her mum.

Mandy lay the cat on her bed. 'So, little watery cat. We'll call you Flicker. I hope you like your new name.' She slipped under her duvet and curled herself around the warm cat's body.

'She ought to feel quite safe and cosy now,' smiled Mrs Hope. She turned to go. 'Sleep well, both of you.'

Darkness flooded Mandy's room as Mrs Hope went out, taking the lantern with her. Soon, Mandy couldn't even see her hand in front of her as she gently smoothed Flicker.

In the blackness of the night, the silence in the old house seemed even deeper. But suddenly the quiet was broken by a mournful miaow.

'It's all right, Flicker,' crooned Mandy, drawing the cat closer to her.

But Flicker could not be consoled. She miaowed again, this time more woefully.

'You're safe,' Mandy said in a calm, reassuring voice. But she could tell that Flicker didn't feel at all safe. Against her chest, Mandy could feel the cat's heart beating rapidly. 'What's the matter, Flicker? Is there something there?' Mandy asked. Perhaps, being able to see in the dark, the cat had spotted something that had frightened her. After all, she'd just been through a horrible ordeal, so anything strange would be sure to upset her.

Mandy sat up and felt in her bedside drawer for the torch she always kept there. All the while, Flicker kept up her pitiful mewing.

Finding the torch, Mandy switched it on and flashed it around the room. At the same time, Flicker stopped miaowing.

'See. Nothing scary in here,' Mandy said, switching off the torch and lying down again.

Flicker responded with another pitiful cry.

'I promise you there's nothing to be frightened of,' Mandy sighed, reaching for the torch once more. 'But let's have one more look to make sure.'

Again, Flicker's cries stopped when Mandy shone the beam around the room.

Suddenly Mandy realised what the problem was. 'Poor little Flicker. You don't like the dark!'

she breathed. 'I guess it reminds you of what it was like in that barrel. Well, Mum's got the lantern and we can't leave the torch on all night because we need to save the batteries. But don't worry, I'll sort out something else for you.'

She slid out of bed and made her way down to the kitchen. *I'm getting pretty good at this*, she thought to herself with a smile as she felt around in the dark for one of the candles that had been burning just a short while ago. She found

one on the worktop then ran her hand along the window sill until she came across the box of matches she'd left there earlier.

Mandy lit the candle then took an empty glass jar out of a cupboard. 'This should do the trick,' she said, letting some wax drip into the bottom of the jar. Carefully, she pushed the candle into the molten wax then hurried back upstairs.

'Look what I've made for you, Flicker,' she whispered as she tiptoed into her bedroom. She put the jar on the bedside table. 'It's a night light.'

Mandy switched off the torch which she'd left on for Flicker while she was downstairs, then slid under her warm duvet. The makeshift night light gave off a comforting glow. 'What do you think of that, Flicker?' Mandy asked quietly.

The timid cat looked at Mandy, her eyes reflecting the soft yellow candlelight. She blinked then opened her mouth in a wide yawn.

'You're exhausted,' Mandy said, smoothing Flicker's silky coat. 'It's been a long, frightening night for you, hasn't it?'

Flicker blinked again, this time very slowly as if her eyelids had grown heavy and she was battling to keep them open. She forced her eyes open again, but only for a moment before she gave in and allowed them to close. And then, at last, to Mandy's delight, Flicker curled herself up into a tight little ball and fell asleep.

Five

A solid blob of wax at the bottom of the jar was all that was left of the night light when Mandy woke up in the morning. Flicker was still curled up against her, fast asleep. *Just as well she didn't wake up when the candle burnt down,* Mandy thought. *I might have had to make another night light in a hurry.*

As she inched herself out of bed, she tried not to disturb the cat. But Flicker seemed to feel her moving and woke with a start. She shook her head then stared at Mandy with a startled look on her face.

'It's all right,' Mandy said, putting out her hand to stroke Flicker. 'It's me, remember? The one who rescued you from the water.'

Flicker shrank back from Mandy's hand and sat huddled up, watching her suspiciously.

'You're really timid, aren't you?' Mandy murmured, moving slowly away from Flicker. 'Don't worry, I'll leave you alone for a while. I'm sure you'll soon get used to me.'

She dressed then closed her bedroom door before going downstairs. Flicker had had one lucky escape already. But she might not be so fortunate if she slipped out of the house and ended up in the flood water again.

'How's Flicker this morning?' asked Mrs Hope, meeting Mandy at the bottom of the stairs.

'Awake but very nervous,' Mandy answered. 'So I don't think we should move her to the residential unit yet.'

Mrs Hope nodded. 'You're probably right. We'll give her time to settle down first.'

Mandy collected a litter tray and some food for Flicker then went back upstairs to her bedroom.

Flicker was sitting on the table under the window, looking down at the flooded garden. As soon as she heard the door open, she leaped to the ground and hid under the table.

'It's only me,' Mandy said quietly as she put the litter box on the floor near the door.

Flicker looked out at her from under the table, her eyes wide with distrust.

'And I've brought you some breakfast,' Mandy went on, crouching down and carefully sliding the dish towards the cat.

Flicker eyed the food but made no move towards it.

'I bet you're starving,' Mandy said. 'But you're not going to eat until I leave, are you?' She straightened up then left Flicker alone again and went to see to Stardust.

She was washing out the chinchilla's water dish when Mr Hope came into the kitchen. 'Want to come with me to check on Scraps?' he asked her. 'I could do with some help rowing.'

'OK,' Mandy said, pleased to be able to visit her old friend again so soon.

'I'm going to try to get to Garland's Farm as well,' said Mr Hope. 'Ivor Garland rang to say that Mr Wimberley won't be able to check on the heifer today because there's an emergency on another farm. A flock of sheep is marooned in the fells. But the cow still needs treatment.'

'No wonder you need a rowing companion,' smiled Mandy.

They were preparing to leave when James rang up. 'It's really boring for Blackie, being cooped up indoors like this,' he told Mandy. 'He's driving us all crazy.'

Blackie was James's very lively black Labrador. Mandy knew just how frustrated he would be at having to stay inside for so long. Blackie had so much energy that even after a long walk, he still had plenty of bounce left in him. 'Why don't you let him go out for a swim?' she joked.

'I have. By accident!' groaned James. 'When I came in with the shopping yesterday, he slipped out of the door. Next thing I knew, he was paddling down the road!'

Mandy could picture the scene – Blackie swimming madly away and James yelling at him to come back. 'How did you get him to come home?' she asked curiously. Blackie was well known for ignoring James when he called him.

'I had to go after him in my dinghy and lure him back with some dog biscuits!' James explained. 'He was grinning from ear to ear by the time we got home! I think he thought it was all a big game. But he wasn't too happy when Mum made him stay on the porch until he was dry.'

'We had a soggy animal in our house last night too,' Mandy said. She told James about Flicker. 'No one's rung up about a missing cat so far,' she continued. 'So it looks like we might have to start looking for her owner.'

'That won't exactly be easy right now,' said James. 'But I tell you what. I'm taking the dinghy to fetch some more things from the post office this morning. If I tell Mrs McFarlane about Flicker, she can tell everyone she sees.'

'Good idea,' Mandy said. 'And we might even bump into you again. Dad and I are going out in the boat in a minute to see Scraps.'

The journey to Walter's cottage was easier now that the wind was just a light breeze and the rain was beginning to let up. But the flood water was still very high, submerging all the roads in and around the village. The only way to get anywhere without getting wet was definitely still by boat.

When Mandy and her dad arrived at the

cottage, they found Scraps lying exactly where she'd been the day before. And next to her, as if he hadn't moved either, was Tom.

'It's almost like Tom's guarding her,' said Walter, caressing both cats. His voice was filled with sadness. 'Scraps has had a tiny bit to eat and some water, but that was last night. Since then she's refused everything – even cheese, which she's never turned down before.'

'She's probably still feeling very nauseous,' explained Mr Hope. 'So the last thing she'll want is food. Just keep offering her water.'

'Aye, I've been doing that,' said Walter. He paused as a worried frown spread across his face. 'This kidney trouble she's got . . . it's not, er . . . catching is it?'

Mr Hope shook his head. 'Not at all.'

Walter let out a small sigh of relief. 'It's just that Tom seems to have gone off his food too,' he said.

'I'm sure it's nothing to worry about,' said Adam Hope, looking closely at the tomcat. 'He seems to be in good shape.'

'Is Missie all right?' Mandy asked, glancing around for Walter's other cat.

'She's fine. Fussy as ever but still eating if I give

her what she likes,' said Walter, with a faint smile.

Mandy knelt down and gently scratched Tom under his chin. 'You're probably just being sympathetic and don't want to eat in front of Scraps,' she said.

Mr Hope gave Scraps another injection to help with the nausea, then he and Mandy left Walter stroking the ginger cat over and over, as if he could will his old friend to get better.

In a melancholy mood, they paddled past the marooned pub. The sadness of seeing the old cat nearing the end of her days made everything seem so much more dismal. Mandy could feel the heaviness of the depressing hush that hung over the normally lively village. There was no laughter bubbling out from the pub windows; no cheerful greetings ringing out across the street. Just the sound of the oars swishing as they cut through the water.

Mandy glanced back. Christmas would be very bleak for Walter. *It's going to be bad enough for the rest of us with all the flooding and no electricity*, she thought. *But with Scraps so ill, it's going to be even worse for Walter.*

Lost in thought, Mandy stopped concentrating

on her oar until her father's voice brought her back to reality. 'Watch out, Mandy,' he said loudly. 'You're catching crabs!'

Mandy looked down at her paddle and saw that it was missing the water altogether. 'Sorry, Dad,' she said, correcting her stroke.

'We're going to be paddling upstream to the farm now,' said Mr Hope. 'It'll be hard work with the current flowing against us so you'll need to keep your wits about you.'

Together, they pulled rhythmically on the oars and were soon gliding smoothly through the rushing water.

'At this rate, we'll be champion rowers in no time,' puffed Mr Hope. 'We'll be able to take on anyone in a boat race.'

'Oh yes,' Mandy grinned. 'Like the Oxford and Cambridge teams!'

'Absolutely!' chuckled Mr Hope. 'They wouldn't stand a chance against us.'

A pair of ducks went past them, floating effortlessly on the current. 'They don't look at all put out by the floods,' Mandy observed.

'On the contrary,' grinned Mr Hope. 'They're having a great time.'

The ducks drifted away and were almost out of sight when Mandy heard a high-pitched bark, followed by a yell. Then she saw a dinghy appearing from behind a half-submerged hedge about thirty metres downstream. 'It's James,' she said. 'And Blackie!'

James was sculling hard towards them, with Blackie leaning over the prow, barking at the ducks. The light rubber dinghy pitched and tossed as the big dog bounced up and down excitedly.

'He'll tip the boat over at that rate,' Mandy laughed. 'Or even puncture the rubber with his nails.'

'Sit, Blackie,' commanded James loudly. But Blackie ignored him, finding the ducks much more interesting.

'Need some help?' Mandy called.

'Yes, please – some calming medicine for dogs!' shouted James with a grin.

'Where are you going?' Mandy asked, trying not to upset the rhythm of her stroke.

'I was trying to catch up with you,' said James. 'Where are *you* going?'

'To Garland Farm,' Mandy explained. 'To check on an injured cow. Do you want to come too?'

'I'll try,' said James, grimacing as Blackie sat down heavily, making the dinghy rock from side to side. 'But I might end up *swimming* there!'

Mandy and her dad slowed down until James was only a few metres behind them.

'Phew! It's hard work rowing a heavy lump like Blackie upstream,' panted James.

'You should try rowing Mandy!' chuckled Mr Hope.

Mandy glared playfully at her father. 'You said just now that we made a good team,' she reminded him.

They rowed on out of the village and through a landscape they hardly recognised. There were sheets of silvery water everywhere, some of them stretching almost as far as the eye could see.

'I should think we're almost on a par with the Lake District now,' said Adam Hope, shaking his head in amazement. 'Who'd have thought our little river could burst its banks so dramatically?'

Despite the damp, chilly air, they were all rather hot from the exertion of rowing by the time they reached the farm.

'Just as well the farmhouse is on high ground,' pointed out Adam Hope.

They dragged the two boats out of the water on to a slope in a muddy field. Nearby was a big heap of broken roof timbers and splintered planks.

'That's all that's left of the old barn,' said Mr Hope.

They trudged past the collapsed building and through the soggy pastures towards the farmhouse and the temporary barn that was sheltering Mr Garland's herd of jersey cows.

Blackie seemed delighted to be able to run about on solid land again. He pulled so hard at the end of his lead that he managed to slip his collar. In a split second he was charging off into the distance, his paws kicking up clods of mud behind him.

'Come back, Blackie!' yelled James. He whistled frantically but Blackie was oblivious to James's call. He hurtled away, not once even glancing back at him.

'I guess I'd better go after him,' sighed James, heading out across the field.

'See you in about a year,' Mandy laughed, as Blackie faded to a black dot under the far hedge.

The makeshift barn was a lean-to at the side of

the farmhouse. The farmer had seen the Hopes arriving and came out to meet them.

'Thanks for going to all this trouble to reach us again,' said Mr Garland. 'I really appreciate it, and so will the heifer.'

'It's what we're here for,' smiled Mr Hope as they entered the shed. Inside, eight cows clustered together in the middle, feeding contentedly on a pile of fresh hay. At the far end of the shed, roped off from the others, was the injured heifer.

Mandy noticed at once the deep gashes on her back and shoulders. 'Ouch!' she exclaimed sympathetically. 'Those cuts look really painful.'

'You should have seen how bad they were when I first saw her,' said her dad. He examined the wounds to make sure they hadn't become infected. The heifer flinched as he touched her, but otherwise stood trustingly while Mr Hope attended to her.

Mandy massaged the cow's neck and spoke softly. 'You'll soon be feeling better,' she promised.

Relaxing under the soothing touch, the heifer fixed her big, liquid brown eyes on Mandy. Then she pushed her head forward and gave Mandy a velvety lick right across her face.

'Thanks!' Mandy spluttered, wiping her face. 'Just what I needed – a big wet kiss!'

'Looks like she's feeling a lot better already and she's saying thank you!' laughed the farmer.

Mr Hope prepared a syringe then injected the heifer's rump. 'She may *think* she's feeling better,' he said, vigorously rubbing the spot where the needle had gone in. 'But these wounds will take some time to heal. You're going to have to clean them out every day to make sure no infection sets in,' he advised, giving the farmer a tube of antiseptic ointment.

They left the cow and went outside. James was trudging back across the fields towards them with Blackie straining at the end of his leash.

'Poor James,' Mandy grinned, as he approached them. 'You look worn out.'

'I am,' said James, wiping a few specks of mud off his glasses. 'It's like I've been in some kind of marathon after all that rowing and running!'

'Well, before you start the next leg of the race why don't you all come in for a cup of tea and a mince pie?' Mr Garland asked.

'Sounds good to me,' said Mr Hope.

While they were taking their wellies off on the

porch of the small farmhouse, Mr Garland turned to James. 'Would you mind leaving your dog out here?' he asked him. 'You see, we're a bit full up indoors.'

'Sure,' said James, looping Blackie's leash around a pillar then tying a strong knot in it.

Mandy wondered what Mr Garland meant. She didn't think he had a very big family. But as they went into the cosy kitchen, she quickly understood. The place was full of cats! There were three lying on a mat in front of the cooker, and two sprawled out on the kitchen table. Behind the door, a plump grey cat was curled up in a basket of clean laundry, while another peeped out from behind a box. Mandy thought she'd seen them all until two young tabbies came scampering into the kitchen and began wrestling playfully in front of her.

'You must love cats,' Mandy said, looking round in amazement.

'Oh, I do. Although they're not really pets,' said Mr Garland. 'They're barn cats. But when the building collapsed the other night, I had to bring them in here.'

'Lucky none of them was hurt,' remarked James,

bending down to smooth the cat in the laundry basket.

'Aye. These are all fine,' agreed the farmer. 'But I did lose one of them.' He filled the kettle with water. 'There's been no sign of her since that night. She might have run away in terror, I suppose, or she could even have been washed away.' He lit a match and held it against one of the rings on the gas cooker.

Washed away! The words struck a chord in Mandy. 'Was she a black and white cat?' she asked.

'Yes. A young spayed one, about six months old,' said the farmer, putting the kettle over the flame. 'The sister of those two tabbies playing over there.'

'Did you have any barrels in the barn?' Mandy continued.

'Just one,' replied Mr Garland, looking puzzled. 'Funnily enough, some of the cats liked to sleep in it.'

Mandy was elated. 'Your cat's fine,' she said, smiling broadly. 'She's just a bit scared. And at the moment, she's safe and sound in my bedroom at Animal Ark!'

Six

'Animal Ark?' echoed the farmer, his eyes wide with surprise. 'How on earth did she get there?'

'By barrel!' Mandy smiled. 'I found her floating past our front door.'

The farmer was astounded. 'I'm glad to hear she's OK,' he said, shaking his head slowly from side to side. 'But who would have believed she'd end up on the other side of the village?'

James was frowning as if trying to work something out. He pushed his glasses up his nose and said, 'Actually, it's not that hard to believe. Especially with the river flooding right up to the barn as well as all the way to Animal Ark.'

'Sounds logical,' agreed Mr Hope. 'And when you think how strong both the wind and the current must have been, it's no wonder the barrel travelled such a distance.'

James turned to Mandy. 'Just as well you came here today,' he said. 'Otherwise it might have taken us ages to find out where Flicker came from.'

Mandy was already picturing the happy reunion of the little black and white cat with the others. 'She's going to be so pleased to be back with her own family,' she agreed.

The farmer was pouring boiling water into a teapot. He stopped and turned to Mandy with an uncomfortable look on his face. 'Actually,' he began, then cleared his throat. 'I'm not sure if . . .' He hesitated again. 'You see . . . Well, the thing is, I just don't have the room to take her back,' he said, his words now tumbling out in a rush. 'And with a sick cow and all the repairs I have to do around here, I don't think I'll have the time to care for her properly, especially if she's not well either.'

'But she's not ill,' Mandy protested. 'Just a bit shaken. She'll be fine when she's back where she belongs.'

The farmer shrugged his shoulders. 'I'm very sorry. I just don't think I can fit another animal in here right now. You can see how over-run I am.' He looked at Adam Hope. 'And anyway, I'd already been thinking of trying to find homes for some of the cats. You couldn't find a new owner for her, could you?' he asked hopefully.

Adam Hope tugged at his beard. 'It's hard to say. Everyone's very busy at the moment.'

'And right now, everyone's flooded out,' pointed out James. 'No one's going to want to make things more complicated by taking in a new pet.'

'And what about Flicker's feelings?' Mandy protested, thinking of the cat's timid nature. 'Imagine what it would be like for her, to be pushed from pillar to post after all that's happened. She *deserves* to feel safe and to be with people and cats that she trusts.'

But Mr Garland was adamant. 'I really haven't got the room at the moment,' he insisted. 'And it'll be ages before I can build a new barn.' He pointed to the grey cat in the basket. 'On top of everything, that one's expecting kittens in a week or two.' He looked at Mandy again. 'And like you said, Flicker needs a loving home. I just can't give her that right now.'

Mandy felt a wave of frustration rising in her. *The floods have ruined everything*, she thought angrily. She stared out at the turbulent water rushing past the shattered timbers of the barn. *If I could keep her*, I would, she told herself. But she knew that it wasn't possible. If they took in all the strays and abandoned animals that came to Animal Ark, they'd soon be overwhelmed.

Adam Hope put an arm around Mandy's shoulder. 'Mr Garland has to be practical,' he said kindly. 'And, anyway, I don't think Flicker would welcome another journey across water just now.' He picked up his vet's bag and turned to the farmer. 'Don't worry. We'll look after her for the time being and try to find a home for her.'

'I'll ask round these parts,' said Mr Garland. 'Some of the neighbouring farmers might want a good barn cat.'

On their way down to the boats, Mandy tried to convince herself that it really was in Flicker's best interests to go to a new home. *But it will have to be a very special one*, she told herself. *She's used to a quiet life in the barn and lots of cats as companions.* Mandy thought how shy Flicker was. Most people wanted confident, affectionate cats. Who would be prepared to take on such a timid little creature?

Mandy turned to James. 'Dad's right when he says it's not going to be easy to find a home for Flicker.'

'That means we'd better start looking for one as soon as we can,' said James, dragging his dinghy towards the water.

'Did you tell Mrs McFarlane about Flicker earlier, James?' Mandy asked, as she and her father hauled their boat along too.

'No. I haven't been to the post office yet,' James answered. 'I'll go there now on my way home.' He stopped at the edge of the water and urged Blackie to jump into the dinghy. 'Sit, boy,' he commanded after the dog leaped easily into the boat. 'And keep still this time. You nearly had me in the water when you saw those ducks.'

The Labrador sat, then wagged his tail expectantly.

'And keep those paws still,' added James. 'Those sharp nails of yours could easily puncture the boat.'

'I'm surprised they didn't do that earlier – the way he was clambering all over it,' Mandy remarked. She sized up the dinghy. There was just enough room for another person. 'I think I should come with you to Mrs McFarlane's, seeing as I know what Flicker looks like,' she suggested to James. 'I can write a description of her to put up in the post office.'

'OK,' agreed James. 'Then we'll go back to Animal Ark and you can introduce me to Flicker before I paddle home again.'

Mandy started to climb into the dinghy.

'Hey! This is mutiny,' announced Adam Hope, standing next to the rowing boat with his hands on his hips. 'Abandoning me and my boat like this.'

'It's for a good cause, Dad,' Mandy laughed.

'Good cause, nothing!' he retorted. 'You're supposed to be my galley-slave.'

'Since when?' joked Mandy in return. 'You're forgetting that you called me a heavy lump earlier.'

'Well, we're not going upstream now. We'll be paddling with the current,' said Mr Hope, winking at James. 'And for that, I need some ballast to keep me stable.'

'Then take Blackie,' chuckled James.

'Blackie! Not on your life. He'll keep the boat about as stable as a leaf in a whirlpool,' said Mr Hope, climbing into the boat and picking up the oars. 'I shall just have to go it alone.'

They paddled back along the swollen river. In her mind, Mandy pictured Flicker's barrel being swept along the same route. It was just sheer luck that the raging waters hadn't carried the cat right past Animal Ark, to who knew where.

For a while, the two boats kept abreast of one another, but eventually they drifted apart as the current bore the rowing boat ahead of the heavily laden dinghy.

Mandy and James steered the little rubber boat along, watching out for the flood debris that was being washed downstream. In contrast to the journey out to the farm, Blackie was very well-behaved. He sat motionless in the stern, watching the passing landscape.

'It's just as well that he went running off like that and used up some of his energy,' Mandy said. 'I think he's too tired to move.'

'I wonder about that,' said James, narrowing his eyes as he looked at Blackie. 'If I know him, he's plotting something really big. Like how to make the boat capsize.'

'You wouldn't do a thing like that, would you, Blackie?' Mandy grinned.

Hearing his name, the Labrador suddenly stood up and took a step towards Mandy. The dinghy started rocking wildly.

'See what I mean,' gasped James, pulling up his oar and holding it in front of the dog to stop him moving forward again. 'Sit, Blackie!' he said sternly. '*SIT*!'

Blackie looked at him in surprise, as if he couldn't believe James could be so firm.

'SIT!' James commanded again.

But Blackie remained standing. Then without any warning, he shook himself vigorously, spraying jets of muddy water off his coat and all over Mandy and James.

The dinghy pitched and tossed so violently that water seeped in over the sides.

Mandy dug in her oar, trying to steady the boat. 'Blackie, sit!' she said. At last, the big black dog sat down in the puddle of water that was now swishing about in the bottom of the boat.

James took a deep breath. 'You'll be the end

of me.' He stopped. 'I think we'd better avoid his name until we're on dry land,' he said to Mandy.

Before long, the surging river brought them to the flooded village green.

'I think the water's dropped a bit,' observed Mandy. 'This morning, it was almost up to the top step of the pub. And now you can actually see the next step down.'

'That's right,' agreed James. 'But where's the Christmas tree?' he demanded suddenly, blinking once as if he couldn't believe his eyes.

Mandy stared at where the tree had been anchored just a few hours before. There was no sign of it now. 'It must have been washed away,' she said with disappointment. 'The carol service tomorrow evening isn't going to be the same without a tree to sing around.'

'If there *is* a carol service with all this water about,' James pointed out. 'Even if the water has started going down, there's no way it'll have gone completely by tomorrow night.' He stood his oar upright in the water until the blade touched the ground. The water reached halfway up the paddle. 'See? It must be about half a metre deep still. No one's going to want to stand up to their waists in cold water to sing carols!'

'No carol service, no decorations, no tree, no lights. That means no Christmas, I guess,' Mandy murmured dejectedly.

Then, as if to highlight just how miserable things were, Julian Hardy, the landlord of the Fox and Goose, and his eleven-year-old son, John, came out of the front door and started gathering up the fairy lights. The lights had slipped down from the eaves and were dangling so close to the ground that they were in danger of falling into the water.

Julian saw Mandy and James paddling across the submerged green. He waved to them and called, 'Nice to see some people out and about!' He began winding the string of lights around one arm. 'Pity you weren't here a little earlier. I could have used a dinghy.'

'Why?' asked James, steering the boat closer to the pub.

'To rescue the Christmas tree,' explained John. 'We saw the rope breaking and tried to wade out to grab it, but we were too late. We might have managed if we'd had a boat.'

'I suppose the tree's well on its way to the

North Sea by now,' Mandy said glumly, lifting her oar clear of the water as the dinghy became wedged against a hedge.

'I don't think so,' said James. He was leaning over the side of the boat, scrutinising the water. Blackie leaned across too, as if he were trying to make out what James was looking at.

'Well, at least heading out of Welford then,' Mandy persisted, holding on to Blackie's collar in case he decided to jump into the water. 'And anyway it doesn't really matter, because it's gone.'

James looked round at her. 'It hasn't,' he said. 'It's right here, caught in the hedge. You can just see one branch sticking out of the water.'

Mandy looked to where James was pointing. 'You're right,' she said, seeing the tip of a branch just visible above the water.

Julian craned his neck until he spotted the tree too. 'Well, even if it isn't on its way to Denmark, it's still no good to us like that.'

'It's better than nothing,' said James, trying to sound cheerful.

'We could try and rescue it now,' suggested John.

Julian looked doubtfully at the submerged tree. 'I don't know how, with the current still so strong,' he said.

Mandy and James left the Hardys trying to work out how to salvage the tree and paddled on to the post office. Mandy went in, leaving James in the dinghy with Blackie because dogs weren't allowed inside.

The bell rang cheerfully as Mandy pushed open the door. 'Be with you in a sec!' called Mrs McFarlane from the back.

Mandy heard a door closing then Mrs McFarlane appeared, drying her hands on a towel.

'I've just been sweeping some water off the back porch,' she said. 'Thank goodness the rain's stopped at last. Let's hope that's the end of it now.'

Mandy gave her James's list of groceries then told her about Flicker. 'Could I put a notice up in here asking about a new home for her?' she asked.

'Of course,' said Mrs McFarlane. She gave Mandy a sheet of paper and a felt-tipped pen. 'But there won't exactly be crowds reading it right now. You and James are practically the only customers I've had since the flooding started!'

'But when the flooding is over, there'll be floods of people coming in because they'll have run out of things at home by then,' Mandy smiled. 'And then they'll read about Flicker. Someone's bound to want her.'

'Let's hope so,' said Mrs McFarlane.

While Mandy made the notice, Mrs McFarlane fetched all the items on the list and packed them into several plastic carrier bags. 'Can you manage?' she asked, giving them to Mandy.

'We'll be fine,' Mandy told her, going towards the door. 'As long as Blackie behaves himself.'

After the strenuous row to the farm earlier that day, the short journey from the village to Animal

Ark seemed very easy. Before long, and with their arms aching from the exertion of rowing for most of the morning, the two friends came to the end of the driveway. Mandy looked up as they paddled under the sign and saw a shaft of sunshine and a patch of blue sky in the west. It cheered her up enormously. 'Enough blue sky to make a sailor a new suit,' she smiled, remembering one of her gran's sayings. 'That means it's definitely clearing up.'

'Great!' said James. 'That'll make it easier for us to find a home for Flicker.' He jiggled his oar in the water to get rid of a plastic bag that had become wrapped around the blade. 'I can't wait to meet her.'

'She's really sweet,' Mandy told him. 'But don't forget she's also very shy, so she might not let you go anywhere near her just yet.'

They paddled into the garden and as they neared the house, James stared at the brightly coloured flotilla of rowing boats bobbing about. 'It reminds me of a marina,' he joked. 'I feel like I'm on holiday. Now all we need is some bright sunshine and lots of people . . .' He paused as something dawned on him. 'I've got it!' he burst out. 'We *can* have the carol service after all. We can use the rowing boats to get everyone there!'

'That's a brilliant idea!' Mandy declared, punching the air so enthusiastically that the dinghy reeled and tossed. 'Oops!' she said, holding the sides of the boat as it gradually stopped rocking.

Blackie put his head to one side and looked at her quizzically. 'OK, boy,' Mandy laughed. 'You're not the only one to rock the boat. I'm in the dog house too!' Then, beaming happily at James, she went on, 'I can just imagine what it will be like. We've got enough boats for the whole of Welford to float on the green. Even without the Christmas tree, it'll be the best carol service ever!'

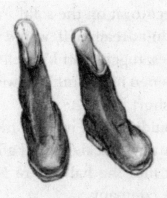

Seven

'We'll have to ask the boat company for permission, of course,' Mandy realised, as they wedged the dinghy against the rowing boat on the front porch.

'Yes. And right now we'd better ask your mum and dad for permission to take Blackie indoors,' added James, holding the dog's collar to stop him plunging off the steps and back into the water. Even though the Labrador had already shaken off a lot of mud and water, his coat was still very damp.

'They won't mind,' Mandy said. 'As long as he

doesn't expect to sit on the sofa!'

'You wouldn't dream of it, would you, Blackie?' grinned James, tugging off his wellies.

Blackie opened his mouth in a wide doggy grin then gave a short bark.

'Butter wouldn't melt in your mouth,' Mandy chuckled, patting Blackie's head affectionately.

They went into the hall where Mandy dialled the boat hire company.

'It's a grand idea,' said Andrew Bond enthusiastically when Mandy explained what they had in mind. 'And I tell you what, I'll come round in one of my other boats to give you a hand. I love a good singsong.'

'Thank you. That's really kind,' Mandy said. She hung up and told James about Mr Bond's offer.

'That will make things easier,' said James as they went through to the kitchen. 'I was wondering how we'd move all the boats by ourselves. Now the next thing is to tell everyone about it.'

'What are you two plotting now?' asked Emily Hope, who was sitting on a chair with Stardust in her lap. She looked at Blackie and frowned, then quickly returned the chinchilla to the safety of her cage. 'Better not take any risks,' she said.

'We're organising a really great carol service,' Mandy said, reaching her fingers through the bars and rubbing Stardust's chest.

Mr Hope was busy making a pile of sandwiches. He looked up from the table and said suspiciously, 'Not on board Animal Ark, I hope.'

'No. On board the rowing boats,' responded James.

'You mean, everyone's going to be floating about our garden singing Christmas carols?' asked Adam Hope, looking confused.

Mandy shook her head. 'No, Dad. They're all going to the village green,' she laughed. 'We'll tow the boats to people and they can row there.'

'It's a terrific idea,' said Mrs Hope. 'But let's hope other people think so too. After all, it's still rather grim outdoors.'

'It's going to be much better tomorrow,' Mandy said positively. Turning to James, she said, 'Come and meet Flicker.'

They left Blackie with Mr and Mrs Hope and went upstairs. Mandy opened her bedroom door cautiously and peeped inside. Flicker was asleep on her bed but sensed Mandy coming in. The timid cat's eyes shot open and she watched warily as Mandy came over to her.

'I see what you mean,' whispered James. 'She really is shy.' He stopped at the door. 'I'll wait here to give her a chance to get used to me.'

'It's all right, Flicker,' Mandy crooned. She sat on the edge of her bed and held a hand out to the cat. Flicker sniffed it hesitantly.

'You're going to have to get a lot braver,' Mandy said, slowly moving her hand forward to smooth the cat. 'Otherwise it'll be really difficult to find you a home.'

Flicker shrank back.

'She's not a very good advertisement for herself,' agreed James quietly from the door.

'No,' Mandy said. 'But I bet she'd be OK if she was with her friends.' She tried once more to touch Flicker. To her surprise, the cat kept still this time and allowed Mandy to stroke her lightly.

'There. That's not so bad, is it?' Mandy said. But she could feel Flicker's muscles tensing as she smoothed her. 'A purr would be an even better reaction,' she said to James. 'Let's see if she'll let you come closer now.'

She kept smoothing Flicker as James

approached. But before James was halfway across the room, the cat suddenly leaped to the floor and dived under the bed.

James shrugged good-naturedly. 'I guess you just need your space at the moment,' he said, then added, 'And we could do with some of those sandwiches your dad was making, Mandy. I'm starving after all that rowing.'

'You're *always* starving,' Mandy teased as they closed the door on Flicker then went downstairs.

Over lunch, the two friends discussed how they'd tell the Welford community about the floating carol service.

'I could ring Gran,' Mandy suggested, going across to Stardust whose cage was safely out of Blackie's reach on the dresser. 'She can tell the Women's Institute about it, and they can tell all their friends.' Mandy's gran, Dorothy Hope, was the chairwoman of the local W.I. and could always be relied on to spread important news.

'And we can row back to the post office after lunch,' said James, 'to put up another notice.'

'I was just going to suggest that myself,' Mandy grinned. 'And I'll take the rowing boat so you don't have to come all the way back here afterwards.' She gave Stardust a carrot, then went back to her place at the table. 'We'll tell Julian Hardy too,' she added, pulling out her chair. 'He might be able to let a few people know.'

'Hold your horses, you two,' said Mr Hope, shaking his head. 'It's all very well to advertise your carols-in-a-rowing-boat service, but we'll need to find out exactly who's coming so that we know who needs a boat.'

'Good point, Dad,' Mandy said. 'I guess everyone will have to ring us up to let us know for sure.'

A look of dismay crossed Mrs Hope's face. 'Get them to ring *here*?' she echoed. 'Not on your life. We need to keep the lines clear in case of emergencies.' As if to underline her point, the phone started ringing.

While Mrs Hope was answering the phone, Mr Hope came up with a suggestion to solve their problem. 'We can ask Gran to be the co-ordinator,' he said. 'You know how efficient she is. People can let her know and she can make a list for us.'

'I'm sure she'll love that,' Mandy said. 'Gran's a great organiser.'

As soon as Mrs Hope came back into the

kitchen, Mandy and James went to ring Gran to put her in the picture.

'Now that sounds like an exciting event,' said Gran at the other end of the line. 'Just what Welford needs after all this miserable weather! I'll get on to it right away,' she promised. 'The Christmas group will be a good bunch to start the ball rolling.' In addition to belonging to the W.I., Gran was also on the committee that organised the Christmas party in the village hall. 'Mrs Ponsonby and the other members are probably expecting to get off lightly this year,' she chuckled merrily. 'I'll have them working the phones in no time at all.'

'Thanks, Gran,' Mandy said. 'We knew we could count on you.'

Back in the kitchen, Mandy and James helped to wash up while Blackie polished off the scraps left over from lunch.

'Nice to have an automatic vacuum cleaner,' smiled Mr Hope, giving Blackie a half-eaten egg sandwich.

'He takes after his owner,' Mandy teased, ducking as James flicked his tea towel at her. Then, looking at her watch, she said, 'We'd better get moving if we're going back to the village. Otherwise I'll end up rowing home in the dark.'

Mrs Hope looked across at Stardust who was nibbling contentedly on the carrot. 'I wonder . . .' she began.

'Yes, love?' prompted Adam Hope.

'Well, that was Stardust's owner on the phone earlier,' said Mrs Hope. 'The family's missing her a lot and would love to have her home for Christmas. But their house is right near the river so even if the water drops a bit, it might be days before they can get here.'

'And you're wondering if I'll take Stardust home in a rowing boat?' Mandy said, reading her mother's thoughts.

Mrs Hope nodded. 'If you put her cage on the seat next to you, she should stay dry,' she said.

'I've got a better idea,' Mandy said, remembering how the barrel had kept Flicker safe the night before. 'We can put her cage inside the plastic laundry basket. Then she won't even see the water around us, let alone get wet.'

Mrs Hope rang up Stardust's owners to tell them the good news, then Mandy and James put

Blackie and Stardust into the two boats and set off for the village.

'It's a proper floating circus,' laughed Adam Hope as the two friends paddled away – James and Blackie in the dinghy and Mandy and Stardust in the rowing boat.

The first stop was Stardust's home. Mandy handed Stardust over to Beth, who was over the moon to have her pet back again.

'Make sure you keep her really warm and dry while all this water's still about,' Mandy advised, before she and James paddled on again.

In the prow of the dinghy, Blackie stood very still, staring straight ahead with an alert expression on his face.

'He looks like a ship's figurehead,' Mandy called across to James.

'Well, I don't trust him to keep still,' said James. 'I bet he's on the lookout for more ducks.' To their relief, no ducks swam across their path and Blackie was still standing calmly when they rowed into the village centre.

As before, Welford was almost deserted. The only people about were Julian and his wife Sara, who was John's step-mother. They were sweeping water away from the front door of the Fox and Goose. When Julian saw them paddling over, he rested his hands on the top of the broom. 'Ahoy there!' he called cheerfully to them. 'Back again so soon! Nothing keeps you two still for long, does it? Not even these floods!'

'Actually, that's why we're back,' Mandy told him. 'We're going to turn the floods into the best Christmas ever!' She outlined their plans for the carol service.

'Now that's what I call a real celebration!' enthused Sara, shaking water from her broom.

'It should be great fun,' agreed Julian. 'I'll tell everyone I speak to.' He glanced over to where the Christmas tree was protruding out of the water and then up to the bare eaves above him. 'Pity about the tree and the fairy lights. But I guess we'll just have to make do without them this year.'

Mandy and James were about to continue to the post office, when they saw the wiry figure of Ernie Bell wading through the water down the lane next to the pub. He was wearing green rubber boots which went all the way to the tops of his legs.

'Those are brilliant wellies,' James called to the

retired carpenter. 'Almost as good as a dinghy for getting around.'

'I found these in a jumble sale back in the summer,' said Mr Bell, his face creased into its usual frown. 'I knew they'd come in handy one day.' He made his way to the front of the pub and sloshed up the stairs to stand next to Julian and Sara.

'How are Sammy and Tiddles?' Mandy asked,

letting her boat drift into the car park where it came to a standstill against a big rhododendron bush.

Sammy was Ernie's pet squirrel which he kept in a run in his back garden, and Tiddles was his kitten.

'They're both fine,' said Ernie. 'Mind you, I had to make a temporary run in my kitchen for Sammy. It's a bit cramped indoors now but I'm luckier than some,' he said, glancing meaningfully back down the lane towards the little cottages where both he and Walter Pickard lived. 'At least all my animals are in good shape.'

Mandy nodded understandingly. 'I suppose we could hope for a miracle for Scraps,' she said, even though she knew the chances of one were very remote.

'Aye. That's what I said to Walter when I popped in on my way here,' said Ernie gravely. 'But he's no fool. He knew I was only trying to cheer him up.'

Mandy sighed and looked down the lane. Tears pricked the corners of her eyes as she thought about poor Scraps. She brushed them away with the back of one hand. 'I don't think anything can cheer him up now,' she said, turning her gaze away from the cottages. 'Not even the carol service.'

'But that's cancelled anyway,' said Ernie.

'Not any more,' said James, who had also drifted into the car park and was holding on to a window sill.

They filled Ernie in about the service. He listened silently then agreed to join in. 'But I won't be here if it starts raining again,' he said grumpily. 'I'm not one for standing about singing in the rain, you know.'

'You won't be standing about,' Mandy corrected him with a smile. 'You'll be floating about.'

'We'll see about that,' muttered Ernie.

Mandy and James's next stop was the post office. As before, James waited outside with Blackie while Mandy went in to tell Mrs McFarlane about their plan, and to put a poster up alongside the one advertising Flicker.

'Now you're sure you won't be back to put up any more notices today?' laughed Mrs McFarlane when Mandy turned to go.

'I hope not,' said Mandy above the jangle of the bell as she opened the door. 'I need a bit of a rest from rowing.'

Satisfied that they'd done as much as they

could to spread the word about the carol service, Mandy and James turned for home.

'I'll phone after lunch tomorrow,' said James. 'By then, your gran should have the list ready for us.'

The two friends then went their separate ways. Darkness was already falling by the time Mandy arrived at Animal Ark. She felt a pang as she approached the dark stone cottage. No warm lights filtered out from the windows to welcome her home. And inside, the only sign that it was nearly Christmas was a drooping artificial tree and a few strings of tinsel.

In the living room, Adam Hope was lighting a fire. 'Mum's upstairs checking on Flicker,' he told Mandy. 'I tried to see to the cat myself, but she wouldn't let me near her.'

'Sounds familiar,' Mandy said. 'She gave James the same treatment.'

She went up to her room. Mrs Hope was crouching on the floor, trying to entice Flicker out from under the bed with a bowl of chicken pieces. There was a new candle in the jar that had served as a nightlight for Flicker the night before. But unlike then, the timid cat no longer seemed to find the light comforting.

'She's not giving an inch,' said Emily Hope, sitting on the floor.

Mandy knelt down next to her. 'She let me stroke her this morning,' she said. 'But she wasn't very happy about it.'

'Perhaps we're putting too much pressure on her,' said Mrs Hope. She stood up and took the dish of chicken over to the other food bowl in the corner. Flicker had barely touched the food that had been there since the morning. 'She might prefer to be entirely alone for a while.'

'You mean put her in the residential unit?' Mandy asked.

'Yes,' said Mrs Hope.

'But she'll be really lonely in there,' Mandy protested. 'At least until we start having patients coming in again.'

'I know,' said Mrs Hope. 'And that's why now's the time to put her in there. Sometimes a traumatised animal just needs a bit of time and space to recover. If we keep pressing her, expecting her to be friendly and happy, she may start feeling hunted.'

Mandy saw the sense in her mother's argument.

If she tried to force the little cat to make friends, Flicker might retreat even further into herself. And then no one would ever give her a home. 'Let's leave her in here for one more night,' she said, still hoping that Flicker might become used to having her around. 'If she's not more confident by the morning, I'll put her in the residential unit.'

Later, while putting fresh sand into the litter tray, Mandy couldn't help wishing that Mr Garland would take Flicker back. It certainly looked like the only solution.

She carried the tray upstairs then stretched out on her stomach and looked at Flicker. The cat stared back out at her from under the bed, her green eyes flashing in the dancing candlelight.

'You're really no trouble at all,' Mandy said softly to her. 'Just a bit shy.'

Flicker twitched her ears and blinked.

'And Mr Garland said you're a really good mouser,' Mandy went on. She stood up and went over to the door then paused and looked back over her shoulder. Flicker was still watching her intently. 'Perhaps when all the flooding is over and things are back to normal, Mr Garland will agree to take you back,' Mandy said. And she resolved right then to do her best to persuade him to let Flicker go home.

Eight

Mandy's heart sank when she drew back the curtains the next morning. It was raining again!

'Oh no!' she groaned. 'This will spoil everything if it goes on all day.' She searched the sky for a break in the low grey clouds, but there wasn't even a hint of blue. *So much for the sailor's new suit,* Mandy thought irritably.

Flicker was also awake. She had spent the night at the foot of the bed but jumped down as soon as Mandy stirred. Now she was hunched over the food bowl in the corner, picking half-heartedly at the contents.

'Come on, Flicker,' Mandy encouraged her in a low voice. 'You can do better than that. You've hardly eaten a thing since you washed up here in your barrel. I bet you're ravenous really.'

But any hunger Flicker had took second place to her anxiety. While she ate, she looked around tensely, her ears pricked for the slightest noise. She was taking no chances. She was clearly poised to flee at any moment.

'Will you *ever* get over your big fright?' Mandy wondered aloud, pulling on some jeans and a thick sweater. She longed to see the cat contented and at ease. And if only she'd let Mandy cuddle her, like she'd done when she was in shock that first night. That would be a big breakthrough. 'Maybe you'll let me pick you up this morning,' Mandy said, slowly going over to her.

But Flicker made it clear that she wanted to be left alone. She allowed Mandy to touch her briefly then she scurried off across the floor to her safe place under the bed.

'You're in real fright-and-flight mode,' Mandy mused. 'It's going to take something very special to get you out of it. In the meantime, we'll let you have your own space.'

After breakfast, Mandy went into the residential unit to prepare a cage for Flicker. She put some clean bedding in one corner then looked around for a cardboard box. *Just in case she feels vulnerable here*, she thought.

She found a suitable box, then lay it on its side in the cage. Next, she chose a fleecy blanket and put it in the box to make a cosy hiding place for Flicker. *It might just remind her of her barrel*, thought Mandy. *Before she was washed away in it.*

When the cage was ready, Mandy went to fetch Flicker. She took a wire cat basket to make sure Flicker didn't escape on her way to her new quarters.

'Sorry to have to do this to you,' Mandy said, reaching under her bed and gently dragging Flicker out. 'But it might be just what you need.'

Flicker wriggled briefly as Mandy lowered her into the basket. But once she was inside, she sat very still and stared out timidly. Mandy carried Flicker downstairs, wishing she could explain things to her. 'You probably think something really horrible is going to happen to you again,' she said.

In the residential unit, Mandy reluctantly transferred Flicker into the cage. 'I'll miss having you in my bedroom,' she said. 'And if you knew what was good for you, you'd miss me too!'

Flicker inspected her new surroundings. She was particularly interested in the cardboard box. She sniffed it inquisitively then, deciding it was safe, crept inside and curled up on the downy blanket.

'All settled?' asked Mandy's father, coming into the residential unit.

Mandy nodded. 'I think so. Now we'll just have to wait and see how she does.'

'In the meantime, there's another cat I need to see,' Mr Hope reminded her.

'Mmm. Scraps,' Mandy said. She peered in at Flicker once more. 'At least there's hope for you,' she said sombrely. 'But the future's not very bright for poor old Scraps.'

'Or for Walter right now,' added Mr Hope as he and Mandy went out of the unit. 'I think deep down he knows it's just a question of deciding on the right moment to put Scraps to sleep.'

'I hope it's not Christmas Day,' Mandy said quietly.

'I'm afraid it'll be sooner than that,' said Mr Hope.

Mandy and her dad went into a treatment room, where Mr Hope replenished his vet's bag. 'I need to ring Mr Garland first to see how the heifer is,' he said, putting some new syringes into the bag. 'Then, assuming I'm not needed at the farm, I'm going to see Scraps. Want to come with me?'

'OK,' said Mandy. 'But do me a favour please, Dad?'

'I will if I can,' answered Mr Hope.

Mandy leaned across the table in the centre of the room. 'See if you can make Mr Garland change his mind about Flicker,' she begged.

Mr Hope shook his head sympathetically. 'I wish I could, love,' he said. 'But you heard what he said. He just doesn't have the space. Not even for one more—'

'One more will make no difference,' Mandy interrupted. 'Especially one that's so quiet and timid.'

'That may be,' said Mr Hope with understanding. He snapped the bag shut and heaved it off the table. 'But you're forgetting one thing.'

'What's that?' Mandy asked, following him into the reception area.

'That a home isn't a good one if an animal isn't

really wanted there,' he said. 'And Flicker is in need of some very special care right now.'

Mandy fell silent. Her dad had a point. Still, things were different with Flicker. For Flicker, home meant being with other cats. *And that's probably another reason she's so timid*, Mandy reasoned to herself. *It's not just her bad experience. She's missing all her friends in the barn. She's not really used to being an only cat.*

Mr Hope picked up the phone.

'Just ask Mr Garland anyway,' Mandy insisted. 'He might want her back after all.'

'I really doubt it,' sighed Mr Hope as he dialled the number and waited for the farmer to answer.

But Mr Garland hadn't changed his mind. After telling Mr Hope that the cow was much better, he asked after Flicker. He was keen to know if anyone was interested in giving her a home yet, but he didn't offer to take her back.

Disappointed, Mandy followed her dad back through the cottage to the front porch. It was still raining but only lightly now. 'Do you think it'll stop by tonight?' she asked as they pulled on their rain gear.

Mr Hope shrugged. 'Who knows? There are

still a lot of clouds about, so it could get worse,' he said, climbing into the rowing boat and picking up an oar.

'Not *worse*,' Mandy protested, settling herself into the boat then slicing her oar into the water. 'Don't even *think* that.'

Paddling away from Animal Ark, she wondered how many more boat trips they'd be making before things were back to normal. She was quite used to getting about on the water now, but there were signs everywhere that the flood waters were receding. On the way to the village, Mandy and her dad saw hedges, low walls and even green stripes of meadow that hadn't been visible in days.

'It'll be great to be able to use motor power instead of muscle power again,' puffed Mr Hope as they rowed past the Fox and Goose towards Walter's cottage.

Arriving, they knocked on the door and Walter called to them to come in. 'The door's not locked,' came his gruff voice.

The atmosphere inside the little house was heavy with sadness. Walter was sitting in a chair in front of the fire with Scraps lying limply in his

lap. Tom sat on the arm of the chair, as if he was guarding his ill companion.

Walter looked up at Mandy and her dad. 'It's good of you to come,' he said, huskily. He rubbed his eyes with one hand. Mandy thought he looked very tired, as if he'd been awake for most of the night.

'Scraps is no better,' continued Walter. 'Is there something else you can give her?'

Mr Hope shook his head sadly. 'We've done all we can,' he said. 'Once the kidneys start failing, there really is no hope.' He bent down and stroked the old cat who looked at him with tired, heavy eyes.

'But she can't go yet!' blurted out Walter. 'She ate a few morsels again during the night. Maybe she's on the mend after all . . .' His voice faded away, and Mandy could tell that he knew in his heart that Scraps wasn't going to get better.

A lump formed in Mandy's throat and she had to turn away. Poor Walter. It was going to be so hard for him to have to make the final decision. *And poor Tom,* she thought. *He looks even more miserable today. He's lost weight, too.*

Mr Hope stood up and put one hand on Walter's shoulder. 'You let us know when you're ready,' he said kindly. 'But don't wait too long. We don't want Scraps to suffer any more than she has to.'

'Aye, I know,' mumbled Walter. 'I just want more time to say goodbye.' He drew the old cat closer as if trying to protect her. 'Sorry to make you go back and forth, Adam,' he said. 'But I just can't bring myself . . .'

'I know,' interrupted Mr Hope sympathetically. 'Don't hesitate to call us at any time. We'll get here as soon as we can.'

'Would you mind having another look at Tom before you go?' asked Walter, stroking the cat with one hand. 'He's worrying me a lot.'

'Still off his food?' asked Mr Hope, picking Tom up.

'Aye. He's had nothing for two days now,' said Walter.

Mr Hope put Tom on the small dining table and examined him thoroughly. 'I can't find anything wrong,' he said finally. 'But cats can be very sensitive creatures. I expect he's feeling too upset about Scraps to want to eat.'

A shadow of anguish passed across Walter's face. 'That means he'll be even worse when Scraps does . . .' He broke off.

Mandy lifted Tom off the table and hugged him to her. 'We're all very sad about Scraps,' she whispered to him. 'But it's very hard for Mr Pickard to have to worry about you too. You must try to eat, for his sake.'

Tom wriggled about until he freed himself from Mandy and jumped to the ground. Then, with an angry flick of his tail, he leaped back on to the arm of Walter's chair and resumed his vigil over Scraps.

Leaving the pitiful scene, Mandy felt very sad. She tried to think ahead to the carol service that night, but the picture of Walter and his two forlorn cats kept forcing itself into her mind.

Back at Animal Ark, Mandy went straight to the residential unit to see if Flicker was any more settled. She knelt down outside the cage and peered into the cardboard box. A pair of bright eyes peered back at her.

Mandy waited, hoping Flicker would venture out to be petted. But Flicker stayed where she was, her wary gaze set firmly on Mandy.

Mandy sat back on her heels. She shook her head and sighed. Flicker, Scraps and Tom – three cats all tearing at her heart strings at once. And right now, it seemed there was no way of helping any of them.

Nine

Mandy was delighted when Grandma Hope told her that lots of people wanted to attend the carol service. 'Just about everyone thinks it's a grand idea,' said Gran when she phoned up after lunch. 'Especially Reverend Hadcroft. He said he'd let the church choir know.'

'Dad's one member who already knows about it,' Mandy chuckled.

Gran read out her list while Mandy jotted down the names. 'Phew!' Mandy said, counting them all quickly. 'I just hope we have enough boats for everyone.'

James arrived in his dinghy after lunch. He'd brought several coiled-up ropes with him. 'I thought these might come in handy for pulling all the boats along,' he said.

'They certainly will,' said Adam Hope. 'All of our ropes are in the garage, and getting them out would mean opening the door and letting the water in.'

'Let's get started,' said Mrs Hope, pulling on her gloves and a woolly hat.

Mandy grabbed her jacket and opened the front door. The light drizzle had finally stopped, and only thick cloud cover remained.

Mandy was about to climb into the dinghy, but she paused as she heard an unfamiliar droning sound coming from somewhere down the lane. 'What's that?' she wondered.

The noise was coming closer.

'It sounds like a motor,' James said, squinting into the distance to see if he could spot what it was.

Emily Hope frowned. 'Surely it's not a car coming up the lane?'

'Not unless it's an amphibious one,' said Mr Hope with a smile.

The mystery was cleared up a moment later. Mandy was the first to see what it was. 'Look!' she exclaimed, pointing down the driveway.

A long motorised punt was gliding into the garden. And steering it through the water to the cottage was Andrew Bond. 'Good afternoon, all,' he called out cheerfully, as he pulled up in front of them and quelled the engine.

'That's a terrific boat,' said James, looking enviously at the powerful engine.

'Yes. I thought it would be more useful than another rowing boat,' said Mr Bond. 'As you can see, there's room for quite a few people in here.'

'It'll be ideal for the choir,' suggested Adam Hope.

'We were just about to rope the boats together,' Emily Hope told Mr Bond. 'And I think we could do with a practised hand.'

'No problem,' replied the boat owner. 'We'll have them strung out behind us in a jiffy.' He picked up a boat hook from the floor of the punt. 'I'll pull them over, Adam, and you can attach them all to each other.'

Before long, there were four strings of brightly coloured rowing boats bobbing about on the water – one each for Mandy, James and Adam and Emily Hope to tow into the village. Andrew Bond double-checked that all the boats were securely fastened, then he went ahead in the punt to collect the choir. Emily Hope had drawn a map for him to show where everyone lived, and put it in a transparent plastic bag to keep dry.

'Let's set sail, everyone,' chuckled Adam Hope. He pushed his oars into the water and struck out towards the lane. With a jerk, his line of little boats lurched off behind him, bumping and knocking against each other in the choppy water.

Mandy set off next. She'd gone only a few metres when she heard the sound of a helicopter flying overhead. She glanced up. The helicopter was low enough for her to see the pilot. He was looking down out of his side window at the scene below him.

'He must wonder what on earth we're up to,' she called over her shoulder to James who was just behind her.

'Yes. It must look really weird,' laughed James.

The helicopter circled once to get another look at the convoy of little boats. Mandy waved at the pilot, who returned her greeting then continued on his way north.

The Hopes and James paddled on, separating eventually to drop off the boats. By the time they had delivered them all, it was starting to get dark. Mandy fetched her friend, Susan Collins, then the two of them rowed to the village green. They found James already there with his mum and dad squashed into the dinghy with him. Mrs Hope appeared soon afterwards, ferrying Mrs Ponsonby along.

'This is just fabulous,' boomed Mrs Ponsonby as other villagers began to arrive. 'Well done, Mandy and James. It's just what Welford needed to put us all back into the Christmas spirit.'

Adam Hope appeared from the other direction with Gran and Grandad Hope. They paddled from boat to boat handing out candles which Gran had brought along. 'Just in case any of you had run out by now,' she said cheerfully.

Last to arrive was the punt carrying the choir. 'Seeing as you're going to lead us all in song, you'd better be in the centre of the congregation,' said Andrew Bond, skilfully manoeuvring the narrow punt into the middle of the cluster of boats.

'Goodness me! We even have a full choir,' exclaimed Mrs Ponsonby. 'Now all we need is some music.'

'That's all arranged,' came a voice from a boat alongside the punt.

Mandy turned. 'It's Mrs Davy,' she smiled. 'And she's brought her violin.'

Eileen Davy was a local music teacher. With her were three other musicians, one a guitar player, the other a flautist and the third, Ernie Bell with his accordion.

'Perfect!' Mandy laughed. She looked around her with satisfaction. For the first time in days, the village green was alive with people. 'It looks almost magical,' she told Susan. 'I wish I'd brought a camera.' Mandy realised that Welford would probably never see another picture like it – dozens of little boats floating about the flooded village green in the midst of winter. And in each boat, sparkling candles shimmered in the darkness, making the black water twinkle with bright points of light.

Reverend Hadcroft welcomed everyone to the service. 'In one sense, it's a most unusual way to hold a carol service,' he said. 'But on the other hand, it's really very appropriate. You see, like Mary and Joseph, we're making the best out of a bad situation. They arrived to find the inn full so they had to opt for an alternative. And as we all know, it was a very good one in the end. Likewise, we found ourselves in a tricky situation too, with a flood that looked set to rival Noah's, but thanks to Mandy and James, we have a wonderful solution.'

There were murmurs of agreement all round, then Reverend Hadcroft continued. 'We'll start with *Silent Night*,' he announced.

The musicians played the opening bars then everyone broke into song. One warbling voice soared above the rest. It was Mrs Ponsonby's. And as she sang, she swayed in time to the rhythm. The result was that the boat she was in lurched and rolled, causing Mrs Hope to hold firmly to the sides.

Mandy caught her mother's eye and they exchanged smiles just as the singing came to an end.

'The next carol is *We Three Kings*,' announced the vicar.

The congregation had just started singing

when Mandy noticed something going on at the
Fox and Goose. Julian and Sara were standing on
the porch, and they seemed to be lighting lots of
tiny candles.

'I wonder why they need so many candles?'
Susan whispered to Mandy.

'And what's John doing?' Mandy whispered
back, noticing him standing a few feet higher in
the twilight gloom than Julian and Sara. 'It looks
like he's up a ladder.'

'Julian and Sara are passing the candles to
him,' Susan pointed out.

'And the candles are in jars with strings tied to
them – a bit like lanterns,' Mandy said. She saw
John carefully position a jar then bend down to
take another candle from Sara. 'It looks like
John's hanging them on to something,' she added.

Gradually, as Mandy and Susan watched, the
candles that John was placing began to form a
triangular outline. Suddenly Mandy realised what
was going on. 'They're putting candles on a
Christmas tree!' she cried in amazement. Quietly
picking up her oars she rowed over for a closer
look.

James had seen it too. He paddled over behind

her. 'It must be the original tree that was washed away!' he whispered.

The singers were on the last verse of the carol. Their voices died down in hushed amazement as the tree took shape before them. Only Mrs Ponsonby continued to sing, her loud voice trilling the hymn's closing words.

'So you salvaged the tree after all?' James called out to the Hardys.

'Yes. The water had dropped so much by this afternoon, that it was quite easy in the end,' called John from the top of the ladder. He stretched up to hang the last jar at the top of the tree, then looked down at Mandy and James. 'It's a bit bedraggled, but you can't really notice that in the dark.'

Everyone cheered and clapped.

'Well done, the Hardys,' boomed out Mrs Ponsonby. 'Welford has its Christmas tree once more. Now we can really celebrate!' She turned to the little band and proclaimed, 'Maestros, play on!'

As the music to *Hark the Herald Angels Sing* rang out around the green, Mrs Ponsonby began conducting all the singers with huge sweeping gestures that made her boat rock even more, so that the water slapped against the sides.

'That's what you call rock and roll carols,' whispered Mandy to Susan.

Later, there was another surprise for everyone – a floating picnic which Grandma Hope and her fellow W.I. members had organised. When the singing was nearly over, Gran held up a big wicker basket. 'Mince pies and shortbread for everyone,' she announced. 'But don't all row across at once. The last thing Welford needs now is a tidal wave!'

'And just in case there isn't enough liquid around, there's hot punch in my boat,' added Mrs Ponsonby, taking several big flasks out of a hamper at her feet.

The singers clustered around the two boats, delighted with the refreshments.

'It's very kind of you,' grunted Ernie Bell, after paddling the band across to Gran and Mrs Ponsonby. Then, with unusual gusto, he held up his cup of punch and toasted the congregation. 'Cheers!' he said. 'And Merry Christmas to you all!'

In reply, a rousing cry of: 'Cheers, everyone!' rang out around the village green.

Mandy had just taken a big bite of her mince pie so she simply held up her cup in a silent toast. As she admired the restored Christmas tree again, she glimpsed the flicker of a candle in the window of one of the cottages just beyond the pub. It was Walter's cottage. *Poor Walter,* Mandy thought sadly. *He would have loved this.*

In her mind's eye, she could picture the old man and his cats. She tried not to dwell on the sad scene, but she couldn't push it from her mind. There was such a contrast between the joy all around her and the sorrow that Walter was going through. *At least Mum and Dad are around for Walter,* Mandy comforted herself. *They'll make sure Scraps goes peacefully.*

There was one more surprise for the carollers that night. As everyone began to sing the final carol the clouds drifted apart and a single star appeared – right above the Christmas tree.

'Well! Who would have believed it?' Mandy whispered to Susan. 'There's a star at the top of the Christmas tree after all!'

Back at Animal Ark later that evening, feeling pleasantly full from several mince pies and a glass of hot fruit punch, Mandy went to check on Flicker.

'It's only me,' she said softly, entering the residential unit which was dimly lit with a gas lamp that hung from a hook in one corner. Automatically, Mandy reached for the light switch on the wall next to the door.

'Oops!' she muttered when nothing happened. It was beginning to feel as if the power would never come back on. She unhooked the lantern and swung it towards Flicker's cage.

Flicker's bright green eyes shone out from inside the cardboard box. But this was all that Mandy could see of her. She knelt down in front of the cage and waited silently for a few minutes. Flicker didn't even stir.

'Oh, well,' Mandy sighed, standing up after a while. 'I guess you still want to be left alone. But it's only two days before Christmas. And no one should be miserable on Christmas Day.'

However, as she spoke the words, Mandy knew in her heart that things weren't always perfect – even at Christmas. *Everywhere, there are people who are lonely or hurting at this time*, she told herself as she went out of the unit. *Just like Walter.*

Ten

When the phone rang early the next morning, Mandy knew before she answered it that the caller was Walter Pickard.

'Would you tell your dad that I think the time has come?' he said gruffly. 'I can't let Scraps suffer any more.'

'We'll be there very soon,' Mandy promised him.

She went into the kitchen to tell her mum and dad. Mrs Hope said she'd go round straightaway as Mr Hope was busy catching up with some paperwork. 'It looks like I'll be able to take the

Land-rover,' she remarked, looking out at the driveway where patches of tarmac now showed between the puddles.

'I'll go with you,' Mandy offered.

While Mrs Hope fetched her vet's bag, Mandy and her dad dragged the compost-filled sacks away from the garage door. The compost had soaked up a lot of water so the bags were very heavy.

'They did a good job,' said Adam Hope, opening the garage door to find only a very shallow layer of water on the floor.

Mrs Hope came out and put her bag into the Land-rover, then she and Mandy drove off. Even though the water was receding, the village was still pretty empty. Mandy spotted just one person hurrying across the soggy green before her mum turned into the lane to Walter's cottage.

The old man must have been watching for them from his front window because just as they pushed open the gate, he came out of the door. Scraps was lying in his arms.

Mrs Hope took one look at the fragile ginger cat and said quietly, 'You're right, Walter. It's time.'

They went inside where Walter sat down in his

armchair. He cradled Scraps lovingly and whispered huskily, 'You're a champion old lass. We've had some good times, haven't we?' Then, as Mrs Hope prepared the injection that would put Scraps out of her pain, Walter lowered his head. 'Goodbye, Scraps,' he said, kissing the cat's head. 'I'm going to miss you so much.'

Tears welled up in Mandy's eyes and she turned away. Out of the corner of her eye, she saw a black and white blur jumping up next to Walter. It was Tom. He was keeping up his vigil while his old companion drifted peacefully into an eternity of sleep.

'There,' Mandy heard her mum saying softly. 'She's gone now, Walter.'

Mandy turned round again. Walter was staring down at the lifeless little body in his lap. He wiped his eyes with the back of one hand and said gruffly, 'I suppose it was for the best. She couldn't have gone on like that any more.'

Mrs Hope nodded. 'And you were with her right to the end. It's the best we can hope for for our pets – to slip away quietly in their own homes surrounded by those who love them.'

'Aye,' murmured Walter.

'I wish we could explain that to Tom,' Mandy said. 'He's really upset.'

Tom was nudging Scraps's limp, silent form with his nose, as if expecting her to wake up.

Mrs Hope stroked Tom's bony back. 'He'll come to terms with things soon,' she said. 'Then he'll probably start eating normally and put back some of the weight he's lost.'

Mandy and her mum waited for a few minutes, then Mrs Hope offered to take Scraps away to bury her.

'I'll be doing that,' Walter said at once. 'I've got a spot all planned out. I know she'd want to stay in her own garden. But I just want to sit with her for a few more minutes.'

Mrs Hope let her hand rest lightly on Walter's shoulder for a moment before she and Mandy slipped away. As they walked down the path, Mandy glanced back over her shoulder. Tom was sitting in the hall window gazing out forlornly at them.

'Poor Tom,' Mandy whispered, biting her lip to fight back the tears that were still welling up inside her.

'I guess he's terribly confused,' said Mrs Hope.

'Some people say that animals have no sense of mortality. But looking at Tom, I'd say he has.'

They climbed into the Land-rover and Mrs Hope started the engine. She looked across at Mandy. 'Try not to worry too much, love. I'm sure Tom will soon go back to being his normal unfriendly self.'

'I don't know,' Mandy said, shaking her head. 'I've never seen him even slightly upset about anything before. I think he'll take ages to get over Scraps.'

That evening, there was another call from Walter. 'I'm sorry to trouble you so late,' began the old man anxiously when Mandy picked up the phone, 'but it's Tom, you see. He seems so ill. It's not just that he's off his food. He's got no energy in him at all. He's just lying on the floor, staring at the fire.' He paused, then added slowly, 'I think he's going the same way as Scraps.'

Mr Hope came into the hall and Mandy handed him the receiver. He listened to Walter, then said, 'We're on our way.'

Mandy and Mr Hope arrived at Walter's cottage to find Tom looking very frail. 'He's definitely worse than he was this morning,' Mandy said, picking him up. The famously bad-tempered cat didn't even struggle in her arms.

'Let's have a good look at him,' said Mr Hope, opening his bag. 'Put him on the table please, Mandy.'

Tom slumped on to his side when Mandy put him down.

'See what I mean,' said Walter. 'He can hardly hold himself up.'

Mr Hope examined Tom while Walter looked on, his face clouded with worry. At last, Mr Hope took off his stethoscope and turned to Walter. 'He's dehydrated and weak from hunger. But I can assure you it's not because of any disease.'

'It's just because he's pining, is it?' asked Walter.

'That's right,' said Mr Hope. 'I can do something about his physical condition, but to be honest, there's nothing I can do to mend his heart. He'll have to come round in his own time. But for now, we'll take him back to the surgery and keep him on a drip for a day or two.'

Mandy wrapped Tom in a blanket, then she and her dad took him back to Animal Ark.

In the surgery, Mr Hope lit a gas lamp. 'Not the

best light for treating an animal,' he said, putting the lamp on the desk, 'but in the absence of electricity, it'll have to do.' He opened a cupboard and took out a plastic bag filled with an electrolyte solution. 'Let's get some fluid into you, Tom,' he said.

While Mandy held Tom still, Mr Hope inserted a needle into the cat's foreleg. Mandy wrapped some sticking plaster tightly round the leg to prevent Tom pulling the drip out. 'Just shows how weak he is,' she said as they took the docile cat through to the residential unit. 'Normally he'd never co-operate like this.'

They put Tom in a cage next to Flicker.

'Some company for you, Flicker,' Mandy said, peering into her cage.

As before, Flicker just stared out from her box. But as Mandy and Mr Hope were about to leave, the nervous cat crept slowly out and sniffed the air. She caught Tom's scent and froze.

Mandy and Mr Hope waited. Flicker lifted her head and looked around. Silently she padded over to the side of her cage, her body tense and her ears pricked. When she spotted the cat in the next-door cage, her eyes grew wide. Then she suddenly turned tail and scampered back to her safe hiding place in the box.

Mandy shrugged. 'She's a real scaredy-cat, isn't she?' she said to her dad.

'Uh-huh. Not the bravest I've ever known,' agreed Mr Hope. He glanced at Tom. 'In fact, the two of them make a very touching pair, seeing as they're both so unhappy.'

The next day, Mandy decided to check the cats before breakfast, so she dressed quickly and went down to the surgery.

'Now look here, you two,' she said approaching the cages. 'It's Christmas Eve so you'd jolly well better cheer up . . .' She stopped. In front of her was a scene Mandy hadn't expected. Flicker was standing at the side of her cage, her nose pressed against the wire. She swished her tail casually from side to side in a way that made her look almost relaxed, and she was gazing at Tom with obvious interest.

'That's better,' Mandy murmured.

Tom seemed to have turned the corner too. Last night, his eyes were sunken into his head and his neck drooped feebly, but today he was

definitely brighter. From where he lay in the middle of his cage, he returned Flicker's gaze, his eyes wide and clear.

'You look a lot stronger,' Mandy told him. She checked the drip to make sure it was still working properly, then fetched some clean water and fresh food for the two cats.

For the first time since she'd arrived at Animal Ark, Flicker seemed to accept Mandy's presence as she moved around. The little cat sat calmly at the wire, alternately watching Mandy and Tom.

Mandy was tempted to make a fuss of her but decided against it. 'I'll wait for you to come to me,' she said. She put clean litter trays in the two cages then went to the back of the room and watched to see what the cats would do next.

The two continued to gaze at each other for a few minutes. Every now and then, Flicker would walk a few paces back and forth, rubbing herself against the wire. Then she'd stop and stare at Tom again. Once she even miaowed softly and pawed at the wire. Tom, in turn, lifted his head and pricked up his ears.

The longer Mandy watched them, the more her hopes grew. Both cats definitely seemed to have begun to recover. *Now all we need is for you both to start eating,* she thought to herself.

Almost as if she'd read Mandy's mind, Flicker glanced over her shoulder at her food bowl. She yawned and stretched then, with a flick of her tail, padded over to the dish and ate every last scrap of food.

That's brilliant! Mandy told herself happily.

Tom took his turn next. Seeing Flicker enjoying her breakfast must have triggered something in him. As soon as Flicker sat back and started cleaning herself, Tom stretched his scrawny neck towards his dish. Still lying on his side, he took a few mouthfuls of the food. Then he pulled himself upright and slowly ate the rest.

'Good boy,' Mandy breathed.

When he'd emptied the bowl, Tom began licking and nibbling at the sticking plaster on his leg that held the drip in place.

'I wonder if he needs that now?' Mandy asked herself.

She hurried into the kitchen where her mum was opening a heap of post, the first to be delivered in days.

'Tom's eaten a whole dish of food,' Mandy told

Emily. 'So he might not need his drip any more.'

By the time Mandy and her mum returned to the unit, Flicker was pushing against the wire again, prodding it from time to time with her paws as if she was trying to get Tom's attention.

Mrs Hope opened the cage, picked up Tom and examined him. 'He's definitely hydrated again,' she said, gently pinching his skin to show how it sprang back healthily. 'So let's get rid of the drip and trust he'll keep eating now.' She removed the needle and plaster, then put Tom back in the cage.

No longer hampered by the drip, the tom cat moved slowly around his cage, inquisitively sniffing the floor and sides. Flicker watched him intently as he came closer to her. She twitched her tail then dabbed at the wire with one paw.

Tom stopped and waved his tail behind him. Flicker pawed the side of the cage again and miaowed softly before pressing her nose against the wire.

Mandy held her breath. Flicker seemed to be giving out friendly signals. Would Tom respond to her?

Tom sat very still for a few moments then stood up and slowly walked across to Flicker. He reached the wire and the two cats touched noses before sitting down and staring at one another, blinking every now and then.

Mandy was wondering how long they'd keep this up when Flicker suddenly sat up on her hind legs and put both front paws against the wire. In reply, Tom stood up and walked slowly along the side of the cage. When Flicker suddenly flopped down and flipped over on to her back, Mandy was delighted. The cats seemed to be accomplishing for each other what no one else had been able to achieve. 'Flicker's calmed down, and Tom looks like a load's been lifted from him,' she said to her mum. 'Why don't we let them out so they can meet properly?'

'I was just thinking that myself,' smiled Mrs Hope.

Mandy took Tom out and put him down outside Flicker's cage.

'Let's allow Flicker to come out by herself,' Mrs Hope said, opening the door to her cage.

Mandy and her mum took a few steps back then waited. With enormous caution, Flicker ventured out into the open. Tom was still rather weak so he sat down. But he kept his eyes fixed on his new friend. Flicker crept up to him, glancing around timidly. The two cats touched noses again, then Tom rubbed his chin against Flicker's face before licking the top of her head.

Mandy beamed at the pair. 'They're definitely the best medicine for each other,' she said to her mum.

'Walter will be so relieved,' said Emily Hope. 'Let's tell him right away.'

They closed the door behind them and went into the reception area. Mrs Hope dialled Walter's number and told him the good news. 'Why don't you come and visit Tom?' she said. 'I'm sure he'll be thrilled to see you.'

Walter lost no time in coming round to Animal Ark. Mandy had hardly finished eating her breakfast when she saw him sloshing across the soggy lawn in his wellington boots. She hurried out to meet him, then showed him into the residential unit. The two cats were curled up next to each other in Tom's cage.

Walter could hardly believe the change in Tom. 'He's back to his old self,' he declared, smiling.

'Not really,' Mandy said.

Walter's smile disappeared. 'You mean he's still in a bad way?' he frowned.

'Well, he's still quite weak and low in body fat,' put in Mr Hope who'd also come in to see how the cats were doing. 'But what I think Mandy means is that he's a changed character.'

Walter's forehead wrinkled into a deeper frown. 'Changed? How?'

'He just seems so much friendlier,' Mandy said. 'Look how he's allowing Flicker to lie so close to him. It's like he knew she needed a friend.'

'Aye. Just like he needed one too after . . .' He paused then said softly, 'after losing Scraps.' He reached into the cage and smoothed Tom, his big hand also touching Flicker.

The young cat opened her eyes lazily and looked straight into Walter's unfamiliar face. Then she did something that delighted Mandy almost more than anything else so far. She began to purr, a clear sign to Mandy that she was finally coming out of her shell.

At first it was just a faint rumble but as Walter continued to stroke the two cats, the purr grew louder and more intense.

A longing look settled on Walter's face. 'Scraps

had a purr just like that,' he said hoarsely.

Walter spent another half an hour with the cats then gave Tom a final cuddle. The tom cat needed to stay at Animal Ark for another day so that he could completely regain his strength. 'I'll be back for him first thing in the morning,' Walter said in the reception area, adding quickly, 'You don't mind if I disturb you on Christmas Day?'

'Not at all,' said Mrs Hope. 'We wouldn't want you to be without Tom for Christmas.'

'That's kind of you,' said Walter.

Mandy leaned against the window and watched the old man heading back down the driveway. She was really pleased that Tom was going home. 'But what about Flicker?' she murmured to herself. 'Just when she's feeling happy and has found a friend, she's about to lose him.'

Mr Hope overheard her. He came across and put his arm around her shoulders. 'I dare say someone will give her a home eventually,' he said.

'It would be lovely if Walter took her in,' Mandy said quietly.

'Unfortunately, things don't always work out

the way we want them to,' said Mr Hope sympathetically. 'Walter won't be ready to take in another cat for quite a while. He needs to get over losing Scraps first.'

'I know,' muttered Mandy, feeling a wave of disappointment for Flicker. 'But perhaps if we persuade him . . .'

'No. This is no time to be pestering Walter,' said Mr Hope firmly.

Christmas morning brought with it a dazzling blue sky and soft, golden sunshine. 'It's just perfect,' Mandy said to her parents over breakfast. 'Except for one thing.'

'What's that?' asked Mrs Hope.

'Flicker and Tom are going to be separated,' Mandy answered glumly.

The moment Mandy dreaded came all too soon. Walter arrived while she was feeding the cats. He waited while Tom ate, then opened the cage. 'Home time, my boy,' he said. 'Missie's going to be glad to have you back. She's been a bit lonely all on her own.'

Mandy caught her mum's eye. Mrs Hope frowned at her and shook her head. But Mandy's main concern was for Flicker. She'd never forgive herself if she didn't at least *try* to keep the two cats together. 'Wouldn't you like to take Flicker home too?' she blurted out to Walter.

'Me?' said Walter, taken aback. 'Oh, I don't think so. It wouldn't be right, replacing Scraps already.'

'You wouldn't be replacing her,' Mandy insisted. 'Nothing can *ever* replace a pet. But you would be helping a cat who really deserves to be happy. And you're the only one she's responded to so far.' Quickly, she outlined what had happened to Flicker.

Walter was surprised to hear all that Flicker had been through. 'You've had a lucky escape, young lady,' he murmured, reaching into the cage and stroking Flicker's head. He fell silent for a minute.

Mandy crossed her fingers, hardly daring to breathe. *Oh, please say you'll have her*, she silently willed him.

'No. It just wouldn't be right,' Walter said finally. 'I can't be forgetting about Scraps so soon.' He stopped stroking Flicker and picked up Tom.

Mandy's heart dropped. 'But you won't ever forget Scraps. And anyway, what about Tom?' she urged.

Walter frowned as he stood up with Tom in his arms. At that point, Mrs Hope stepped in. 'I think Walter's made up his mind, Mandy,' she said. 'And I'm sure Flicker will find a suitable home.'

Mandy turned away, tears stinging her eyes. Flicker was going to be heartbroken. But just as Mandy had given up hope that Christmas would turn out well for Flicker too, Walter cleared his throat. 'I was just thinking . . .' he began, and paused. 'Well, if I know Scraps, she'd want Tom and Flicker to be happy.'

Mandy spun round.

Walter bent down, and reached into the cage again, picking up Flicker. Kindness filled his voice as he spoke. 'Perhaps Flicker should come home with us after all. There's just something about her. Something that makes me think we're meant for her.'

Mandy threw her arms around the old man. 'Thank you!' she cried, hugging both him and the two cats in his arms. She turned and smiled broadly at her parents. 'Now Christmas *will* be perfect,' she said.

Mrs Hope offered to run Walter and the cats home in the Land-rover, but the old man said he'd prefer to walk. 'It's such a lovely day,' he said. 'I could do with a bit of sun on my back. But perhaps Mandy would like to carry one of my cats for me.'

'You bet!' said Mandy.

Soon Mandy and Walter, each with a cat in their arms, set off down the lane. When they came to the Fox and Goose, they saw James and John Hardy in the car park. They were looking up at the fairy lights which had been strung back up along the eaves.

Mandy called out to them. 'Expecting the electricity to come back on soon?' she laughed.

'It has to, eventually,' called back John. 'We thought we'd look on the bright side. That's why James and I put the lights up again.'

James noticed the two cats and came over to Mandy and Walter. 'What's going on?' he asked.

'Flicker's all right now,' Mandy smiled. 'And thanks to Walter and Tom, she's got a new home.'

Mandy could see that James understood at once what had happened. He stroked both cats, then looked at Walter and beamed at him. 'Happy Christmas, Mr Pickard,' he said.

'And Happy Christmas to you,' said Walter.

'May I come and see Flicker settling in to her new home?' James asked the old man.

'Of course,' replied Walter.

The three of them turned into the lane leading to Walter's cottage. Suddenly they heard a shout from John.

'Hooray!' he cried.

Mandy spun round. The colourful string of fairy lights was glowing brightly all around the eaves of the pub! 'Hooray!' she echoed. 'The lights are on at last.'

Siamese
in the
Sun

One

'Oh, it's tiny!' cried Mandy Hope, pressing her forehead to the plane's window. 'Much smaller than I thought it would be. Look, James.'

'Where?' James Hunter, Mandy's best friend, strained against his seatbelt to get his first glimpse of the island of Jersey. He and Mandy had been waiting for the aircraft to break through the cotton-wool layer of cloud carpeted below them. Now it had, and James gave a small whoop. 'I see it!'

The little island floated in a sun-drenched sea of bright blue. Mandy could see the Atlantic Ocean rushing up long sandy beaches and swirling into coves. Rocky cliffs gave way to fields of neat green farmland among neat seaside towns. It looked like the perfect place for a holiday.

'Mum!' Mandy called across the aisle to her mother. Emily Hope looked up from the book she was reading. 'The island is so beautiful!'

'Great, isn't it?' agreed her father, Adam Hope, who had the window seat beside Mandy's mum. 'It's only nine miles by five, yet about eighty thousand people live on it.'

Mrs Hope rubbed her arms and began to gather up her stack of papers. 'Not long now.' She smiled at Mandy, then, as the plane banked sharply to turn, her hand shot out to steady a large book propped open on her tray table.

'Would you put your tray table in the upright position for landing, please?' a passing flight attendant asked Mrs Hope. Mandy's mum nodded, smiling, and started filing her papers into a leather briefcase at her feet.

Mandy turned back to watch the horizon tilt as the plane swooped lower for landing. She was finding it hard to sit still. She and James had spent the flight looking at pictures of the most unusual cat breeds in the books Mrs Hope had brought with her. Mandy's mum was going to be the official vet at a prestigious annual cat show and she was using all her spare time to read up on different breeds and ailments. Names like Russian Blue, Foreign White, Balinese and Siamese, Tonkinese and Ragdoll swirled in Mandy's head, until she felt as if she knew more about cats than most people!

'Surfers!' James said excitedly. 'See, Mandy? It would be brilliant if we could hire some boards.' Mandy and James shared great memories of boogie-boarding in Cornwall one summer.

'Don't worry, we're going to have time to do and see everything,' Mandy replied happily. She scooped back her fair hair into a hasty ponytail. This was going to be a holiday with an added bonus: they were going to be staying at a veterinary surgery which would give animal-mad Mandy a chance to meet some four-legged locals, too!

Mandy's parents were both vets who ran their own busy surgery called Animal Ark in Welford, Yorkshire. For one week of the summer holidays, Mr and Mrs Hope had agreed to take over a veterinary practice in the Jersey village of Beaumont which was run by old friends, Colin and Anna MacLeod. Mandy knew that Mr and Mrs

MacLeod were away in Italy at a veterinary conference, and had left their son, Craig, at home to be cared for temporarily by Mandy's parents.

'I wonder what he'll be like,' Mandy said aloud, her nose to the window.

'Who?' asked James.

'You know . . . James and Anna's son. Craig.' The only thing she could remember about the boy who'd come to visit nine years ago when she was three years old was that they had found a plump, pink earthworm and played with it in the garden.

James wasn't listening. 'Look at those waves!'

'I hope he'll show us around,' Mandy went on. 'One thing's for sure, he'll be as crazy about animals as we both are, so we'll definitely have something in common.'

'Who?' James said again maddeningly, propping his elbow on the arm-rest as he leaned across Mandy to peer down at the golden stretch of sand below.

'It doesn't matter,' Mandy laughed. She clearly wasn't going to be able to compete with the prospect of some seriously good surf, so she gave her full attention to the ground rushing up to meet them. As the plane dipped lower, she spotted a field of emerald green, dotted about with golden-brown cows.

'Jerseys!' she exclaimed. 'My favourite breed of cow. They have the best faces.'

'Another great beach! It must be low tide,' James chipped in. 'You know, I read that Jersey has one of the highest tidal ranges in the world – up to twelve metres.'

'Wow,' said Mandy, impressed. She gripped the arm-rests of her seat as the plane gave a sudden sharp lurch and the wheels thudded on to the runway. She strained against her seat belt as the plane braked hard.

'We're here!' she announced, smiling broadly at her father. Adam Hope gave her a thumbs-up sign from across the aisle of the plane.

They were soon inside the airport terminal, a low, concrete building buzzing with holidaymakers. Small children milled around, clutching bucket and spade sets and inflatable swim-rings, calling to one another in high-pitched voices. The scent of sun lotion wafted in the air. James hurried off to find a luggage trolley and helped load it up.

'Honestly!' Adam Hope grumbled playfully, grabbing suitcases as they cruised by on the conveyor belt. 'You'd think we were staying a year, not a week!'

'That's mine.' Emily Hope lunged for her own case and swung it to the floor. 'And that's it, Adam.'

'Thank goodness for that,' Mr Hope remarked, steadying the teetering pile.

'Look,' said James, prodding Mandy to get her attention and pointing. A woman standing on Mandy's left was pushing a trolley holding a pet's travelling basket. A fluffy white poodle was crouched inside. The dog's immaculate coat had been groomed to a snowy frizz around its small pointed face and it wore a small tartan jacket. As soon as its owner stopped the trolley by the conveyor belt, it began a high-pitched, excited whining.

'There, there, darling Fifi!' The woman bent down and fumbled to open the basket. 'Did you have a good flight, poppet?'

'I wish I could have brought Blackie along,' said James, suddenly looking a bit gloomy.

Mandy linked arms with him. 'He'll be far happier home in Welford, chasing rabbits.'

'You're right,' James said. 'But it would have been fun to have him with us.'

Mandy tugged James along as her dad set off with the trolley. 'Besides,' she reminded him, 'there'll be all sorts of animals to keep us busy at the MacLeod surgery.'

Up ahead, Mandy's parents were waving at a young woman who was holding a placard. On it was written "The Hope Family" in bright red letters.

'Over here!' Adam Hope called. The woman waved back and came over, holding out her hand.

'I'm Jennifer Locke, Colin and Anna's receptionist. I'm glad I found you. Mid-July is the height of our tourist season and the island is packed – hence the crowds!'

'This is Mandy, our daughter,' Mr Hope told her. 'And James Hunter, Mandy's friend.'

'Welcome, all of you,' Jennifer smiled. 'Colin and Anna are so glad you were able to take time to be here. Come on, let's get out of this crush.'

As Jennifer turned to lead them to the car park, she almost collided with the bulging red eyes of a huge inflatable dragon. Short bare legs stuck out from underneath it, and a distinct giggle came from behind the dragon's ferocious head.

'Oops!' gasped Jennifer.

'Sorry,' said a harassed-looking man who was

standing a short distance away. 'Tommy! Come here – now!' The dragon bobbed unsteadily away, still giggling.

Jennifer strode ahead with her hands deep in the pockets of her jeans, her long plait of glossy black hair swinging. As Mandy hurried along behind her, she noticed a post announcing the island's forthcoming cat show and pointed it out to her mother. Emily Hope nodded and smiled, but she was too breathless from carrying her hand luggage to reply.

Jennifer's car was a spacious, rather battered-looking van, with plenty of room for the five of them and their luggage. She steered the van along a road that clung to the coastline, allowing them dramatic views of chalky cliffs carved out by the strong Atlantic tides.

'What a wonderful place,' Mandy said.

'Yes, beautiful, isn't it?' Mr Hope agreed, nodding enthusiastically.

Just then, Mandy spotted a slate sign propped against a boulder on the side of the road. 'Cream Teas'. She turned to grin at James.

He patted his tummy. 'Hmm, yum,' he said.

Jennifer laughed. 'There'll be plenty of time for

those, I'm sure. This,' she went on, 'is St Austin's Bay, our nearest beach. Beaumont is just around the next bend.'

As the village came into view, Mandy felt excitement fizz inside her. Pretty terraced houses, brightly painted, shared the beachfront road with a row of shops. Jennifer eased the van carefully past an ice-cream stall that had attracted a crowd of people in swimming suits. Mandy spotted a village shop, a small café and a bookstore before they turned into the driveway of MacLeod's Veterinary Surgery. It was an old whitewashed building, the top half of which, Jennifer pointed out, was where the MacLeods lived.

As soon as the van stopped, Mandy got out, eager to explore. James heaved his small suitcase out of the boot and Mandy's father wrestled with the rest of the luggage. Jennifer led them around the building to a side door. Behind the surgery was a garden, and Mandy saw a goalpost at the far end of the lawn.

'Will Craig be here?' she asked.

Jennifer glanced at her watch. 'He should be around, though he might be at football practice. Let's go inside and see.'

Inside, Jennifer led them into a pleasant sitting room. Mandy was suddenly hopeful that there might be a cat curled into one of the big, soft chairs, but she couldn't see one.

Upstairs, Jennifer directed Mandy's parents to Mr and Mrs MacLeod's room, then led Mandy and James further along the hall.

'We hoped you'd be OK here, James?' she said, opening the door to a small study lined with bookshelves and with a neat computer table under the window. An inflatable mattress took up most of the floor space, with a sleeping bag on top. 'It's the study, really, but we didn't have any other spare rooms,' Jennifer added apologetically.

'It's fine, thanks.' James looked pleased and Mandy laughed.

'This doesn't mean you can surf the Internet by night as well as waves by day!' she joked.

'Mandy's over here,' Jennifer went on, stepping across the hall to open another door.

'Oh, it's lovely!' Mandy exclaimed, stepping into a sunny little bedroom that overlooked the bay. She put her suitcase down and went to the window. The waves shone like glass in the mid-morning sun. 'Thank you, Jennifer,' she said.

'It's going to be fun having you here. Now, let's see if Craig is around,' she said.

They followed her up yet another flight of stairs to a tiny, third-floor landing. Jennifer knocked on the only door Mandy could see. 'Craig?' she called softly. 'Are you there?'

There was no reply, so Jennifer opened the door. Mandy peered past her shoulder. The walls of the small room were draped in the blue and white colours of a football team announced as Kilmarnock on one of the many banners, and there were posters of soccer players everywhere. A dark-haired boy was lying on his back on the bed, reading a magazine.

'Oh! Hi,' said Jennifer. 'I'm sorry to burst in on you. I didn't know if you were here or not. I wanted you to meet Mandy, and James.'

Craig didn't move, not even lifting his head off the pillow to look at the visitors. Mandy shifted uncomfortably and glanced over her shoulder at James. Craig must be really shy!

'Hi,' she offered, looking back into the room.

'Nice to meet you,' James added, standing on tiptoe to look past Mandy and Jennifer.

Craig looked up and raised his eyebrows at the

three of them. Then he went back to his magazine without saying a word.

'Well . . . we'll see you later, I expect,' Jennifer said cheerfully. 'Sorry to have disturbed you.' She turned and smiled at Mandy and James. 'Right! That's the tour. Do you two want to unpack, or can I get you a drink?'

Mandy spoke for them both. 'Please could we see the surgery now?'

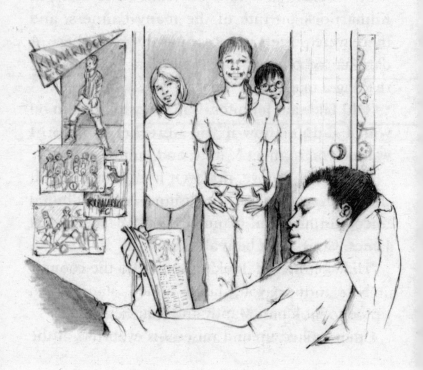

'Sure! Are both of you mad about animals?' Jennifer asked, going down the stairs.

'Absolutely,' James assured her.

'Crazy,' Mandy agreed. 'I really hope I'll be a vet one day.'

'Well, I can't say I'm surprised,' Jennifer chuckled. 'After all, with both parents as vets, you must have had a lot to do with animals.'

'Yup,' Mandy grinned, jumping the last two steps.

She followed Jennifer across the carpeted hall to a door leading to the clinic. The clean, scrubbed smell of the linoleum flooring in the reception area reminded her instantly of home. Mr and Mrs Hope were poring over a stack of files behind the desk and to the right of that was a door marked Residential Unit. Straight ahead were two treatment rooms. It was similar in layout to Animal Ark, only a bit smaller.

'I'm going to go and give your mum and dad a hand settling in,' said Jennifer. 'I'll leave you to look around.'

'Would it be OK if we went into the residential unit?' Mandy asked.

'Sure,' said Jennifer. 'Help yourself.'

Opening the door cautiously, Mandy looked

around the large, airy room. There was a row of cages along one wall.

'Oh, look, James, there's a puppy!' Mandy spoke quietly because the pup was asleep.

'Cute!' said James. 'It looks like a Labrador.' He read the pup's name in neat handwriting on a small chart propped up at the door. 'Rosco.'

Mandy put a finger in through the bars to stroke one soft, floppy ear. Rosco woke up and yawned, then rolled on to his back, showing off a plump, pink tummy and a small stitched scar. He took Mandy's finger in his mouth and began to chew sleepily, wagging his tail.

'Ouch,' she said. 'Needle-sharp teeth, but you're still a sweetie!' She gently withdrew her hand. 'We'll come and spend time with you tomorrow,' she promised.

A beautiful, silvery lop-eared rabbit called Lucky occupied another of the cages.

'It's a buck rabbit,' observed James. 'Look how long his teeth are!'

'That's probably why he's here,' Mandy said. 'Mum or Dad'll have to trim them back a bit, I expect.'

'Here's another dog.' James bent to peer into

one of the lower enclosures. The wiry-haired terrier was deeply asleep and hardly stirred when Mandy read out her name.

'Penny,' Mandy read. 'Hello there.' But Penny was soundly asleep, and didn't stir at the sound of voices.

Next, they fussed over a little mongrel called Fudge, with a bandaged leg, who thrust his muzzle through the bars to lick at their hands, and then introduced themselves to a plump tabby cat called Alice. Alice had a small shaved area of stitches on one ear, which she kept swiping at with her paw. She seemed grumpy.

'Poor Alice,' Mandy said sympathetically.

'Have you met everyone?' Jennifer poked her head around the door of the unit. 'Isn't Rosco sweet?'

'Gorgeous,' Mandy smiled. 'Can we help with anything?'

'Thanks, but it's all done for this evening, Mandy. I wouldn't say no to a bit of help tomorrow, though.'

'We'd love to,' James grinned. 'Just call on us – any time.'

'What a treat it's going to be having you two here,' said Jennifer.

'Well, I'm sure Craig is just as useful to have around,' remarked Mandy, trying unsuccessfully to stroke Alice.

'Yes, well . . .' Jennifer broke off as Emily Hope came in.

'You'd better unpack, love,' Mandy's mum suggested. 'Dad and I have a patient coming in. We'll have to think about supper quite soon, too.'

'Right,' said Mandy, reluctantly turning away from the animals. 'Come on, James, we'd better get organised. Bye for now, Jennifer.'

Taking a last look around the unit, Mandy felt a little shiver of pleasure. It was great to be having a working holiday, doing the thing she loved best: being with animals.

Later, when Mandy was alone in her bedroom, she sat at the window looking out at the sea. A yellow moon threw a shimmering pathway across the surface of the waves. There was a soft knock at the door.

'Come in,' Mandy said.

James came in, rubbing his tummy. 'I'm sure I won't sleep,' he complained. 'I think I ate too much pasta.'

Mandy laughed. 'Look how gorgeous it is out there, James,' she said. 'Listen, can you hear the gulls?'

'Seagulls? At night-time?' James peered out of the window, looking doubtful. 'Shouldn't they be asleep?'

'Well,' said Mandy, 'it sounds like seagulls to me.'

There was another distinctive cry, high and plaintive – and quite close.

'Hey! You're right. Sounds like there's one in the garden down there,' James commented. He yawned. 'Well, I think I'll try and get some sleep. It'll be a busy day tomorrow.'

When James had gone, Mandy got into bed and turned out the light. She didn't feel in the least homesick, she realised, and wondered if it had something to do with being in a veterinary surgery. It was all very familiar, in spite of being such a distance from Yorkshire. She heard the cry of the gull again. She had to admit it was an odd-sounding birdcall – high-pitched and wailing, like a human baby. Mandy thought of the bird swooping and circling over the dark, restless sea, and then she fell asleep.

Two

Early the following morning, Mandy was woken by the telephone ringing at the bottom of the stairs. She lay in her bed, sleepily watching a breeze lift the curtains at her open window.

'I'm in *Jersey*!' she said aloud, suddenly fully awake. She scrambled out of bed and reached for her shorts and T-shirt.

Outside James's bedroom door, she paused. Her mother's voice reached her from the floor below. 'Yes, we're making ourselves at home, Anna,' she was saying. 'It's so beautiful here on the bay, and the weather is perfect.'

Mandy was about to rap on the door when it opened. James jumped when he saw Mandy standing there.

'What's the matter?' he said, looking worried.

'Nothing!' she responded. 'I was just going to see if you were up.'

'It feels like breakfast time to me,' said James, adjusting his glasses.

'What happened to all that pasta?' Mandy teased, starting down the stairs. She turned back to James. 'Mum's on the phone to Mrs MacLeod,' she added in a whisper.

'Craig?' Mrs Hope said into the receiver. 'Yes, he's here. We didn't see much of him last evening, but we were busy finding our way about. Shall I get him for you?'

Mandy was halfway down the stairs and she waved her hands to get her mother's attention. Mrs Hope looked up.

'I'll get him, shall I, Mum?' Mandy offered.

'Oh, thanks, love.' Emily Hope smiled at James, then went back to her conversation with Anna MacLeod.

Mandy shot back up the stairs to the first floor and on up to Craig's bedroom. It was hot up here, under the roof. Mandy tapped lightly on the door.

'Craig?' she called, suddenly feeling shy. 'It's Mandy. Your mum's on the phone from Italy.'

The door opened abruptly. Craig looked at her. He was wearing a football shirt. 'Yeah?' he said.

'Phone,' Mandy repeated. 'For you.'

'Right,' Craig said, sliding past Mandy. He took the stairs two at a time, landing at the bottom with a great thump.

'He's here, Anna,' said Mandy's mum. 'I'll say goodbye, then. Have a great time – and say hello to Colin.'

Craig took the phone, and Emily Hope ushered Mandy and James out of the hall and into the kitchen.

Adam Hope was sitting at the table, leafing through a fat leather appointment diary. There was a steaming mug of tea in front of him.

'It doesn't look too busy,' he said, 'for a Saturday morning.' He looked up. 'Oh hello, you two! James, you look half-asleep.'

'No, I'm not,' James grinned, quickly combing his tousled hair with his fingers. 'I'm just hungry.'

'Again?' Mrs Hope groaned playfully. 'Well, eat

all you want. Adam's been out to the village shop to buy eggs and bread, and there's cereal.'

'That was Anna on the phone,' she went on, pouring tea from a big brown pot.

'Maple Cross Farm . . .' Mr Hope was reading aloud from the diary and not really paying attention.

'A farm?' Mandy was instantly all ears. 'Are you going there?'

'Just a routine visit – some post-operative stitches due to be removed,' her mum explained.

Adam Hope stopped reading and took a sip from his tea. 'Perhaps we'll arrange to go out on Sunday, Emily? That way we can see some of the island.'

'Oh, great idea, Dad!' Mandy said. 'And we'll be able to see some Jersey cows up close.'

Her father smiled. 'But you've seen Jersey cows before, Mandy. They won't be any different, you know.'

'Oh, yes they will,' Mandy insisted. 'Jersey cows in Yorkshire are just not the same as Jersey cows on Jersey Island.'

Mr Hope laughed. 'I can't argue with that!'

Just then, Craig came into the kitchen and stopped inside the door. For a second, everyone was silent. Then Mrs Hope spoke.

'Hi, Craig. Would you like some breakfast?'

'No, thanks,' he replied. 'I'm off to play a game.'

'Football?' James asked eagerly, crunching on his cornflakes as Craig nodded.

'James is mad about football.' Mandy looked at Craig and playfully rolled her eyes.

'Good,' Craig answered. 'So . . . I'll see you, I expect.'

'But won't you have a glass of—' Emily Hope began, but Craig was out of the back door and into the garden before she could finish her sentence. Mandy looked at James. He was staring after Craig, looking disappointed.

'An eager sportsman,' Adam Hope decided, going back to the appointment diary.

'I suppose it's not surprising if he's shy,' Mandy said. 'It can't be easy, having a whole family suddenly arrive in your home.'

'Still,' said James, glumly, 'I could have gone along with him, if he'd asked.'

'Yes,' Emily Hope agreed. 'That would have been nice. Another time, perhaps, James.'

'Doesn't he help around here?' James added. 'I mean, with the animals?' He nodded in the direction of the surgery on the other side of the kitchen wall.

'It seems not.' Emily Hope shrugged. 'Colin and Anna didn't promise us his help, so we can't really expect him to pitch in.'

'He must earn his pocket money in other ways,' said Adam Hope, but Mandy thought her father looked as surprised by Craig's offhand manner as she was.

Mrs Hope stood up. 'Well, I'm going to go into the surgery now. Mandy, I'm sure you and James would like to help?'

Mandy stood up, sloshing milk from the jug she was holding. 'Of course!' she grinned, reaching for an apple with her free hand. 'Ready, willing and more than able!'

'Good.' Her mum smiled. 'You can start by feeding the animals in the residential unit – but eat something first!'

'I will,' Mandy answered, sinking her teeth into the crunchy apple. She was already at the door, with James hard on her heels.

'Let's go!' he said.

Rosco was having a game with a rubber toy when Mandy and James approached. The puppy's ears shot up happily when he spotted them and he began to scrabble at the bars with both front paws. Mandy slipped the bolt and lifted him into her arms. The pup licked her face, his tail wagging furiously.

'You're adorable,' Mandy told him, smoothing the pale-gold fur on his forehead. Rosco tried to chew on her fingers. She put him on the floor and he tumbled about.

'He's so naughty,' James laughed. 'Let's distract him with breakfast.'

'Good idea,' Mandy said. 'I'll get it.'

Rosco pounced on James's shoelaces and tugged at them, making fierce little growling sounds, while Mandy measured out his morning ration from the recommendation on a little chart hanging on the door. The pup's shiny black nose twitched as he smelled food and he bounced over to the bowl she set down.

Mandy stroked him. 'We'd better clean out his kennel while he's eating,' she said.

'I'll make a start on Penny.' James nodded towards the scruffy little terrier in the kennel adjoining Rosco's. The dog still seemed sleepy, but she perked up when James came close, then began to tremble nervously.

'Don't worry,' James said soothingly, stroking the top of her head. 'The scary part is over, girl. I'm here to make you more comfortable.' He'd helped Mandy in the residential unit of Animal Ark before. Now, he was almost as practised as she was at the routine chores.

Mandy smiled as she stripped Rosco's bedding. He came waddling over to lie curled against her foot and gave a contented sigh.

'How's it going?' asked Emily Hope, coming into the room. She was wearing a white coat that seemed a little too big.

'Fine,' Mandy answered. 'Are you and Dad finding your way around?'

'With Jennifer's help, yes,' her mum said. 'It's a well-organised surgery. We shouldn't have any problems.' She looked at her watch. 'We've got a poodle coming in quite soon.'

'What's up?' Mandy asked.

'The owner said she has a shard of bone embedded in her gum, poor girl,' Mandy's mum replied as she opened a drawer neatly labelled 'surgical gloves'.

'Can Mandy and I take Rosco into the garden?' James asked.

'You can – but not today, James. We don't want
him undoing all the good those stitches are doing
him,' said Mrs Hope, looping a stethoscope around
her neck. 'Now, I've got to go and scrub up. How
about having a walk around the village when
you're finished in here? We could do with some
more milk.'

'Sure,' Mandy said, dropping a kiss on to Rosco's
soft yellow muzzle. 'We'll go off and explore as
soon as we've finished.'

Mandy's mum smiled. 'Thanks, both of you.
You're great assistants, you really are.'

When Lucky, Penny, Fudge and Rosco had been
fed and were back in their cleaned cages, Mandy
and James slipped out through the reception and
on to the street. Mandy waved to Jennifer, who was
talking on the phone.

'Pity we haven't got our bikes,' James remarked,
squinting in the sunlight.

'It's a tiny place!' Mandy said. 'We can walk.
And,' she added, 'we haven't got Blackie tugging
us furiously along after some smell he's picked up.'

James smiled. 'You're right,' he said.

Beaumont village was filled with Saturday

shoppers. Mandy and James walked left out of the surgery car park and a few paces along, Mandy stopped.

'Gibb's Groceries!' she said, her hands on her hips, gazing at the sign. 'It's right next door to the surgery – so Dad didn't have to go far at all this morning.'

'Let's go the other way,' James suggested. 'We can pick up the milk on the way back.'

'OK,' said Mandy.

As they walked along the busy main street, Mandy hoped they would find a turning that would take them to the beach. She could hear the gulls; it couldn't be more than a few minutes' walk. They went on down the street, past small glass-fronted shops and a row of blue and white painted houses. One side of the road opened into a rectangle of smoothly cut grass, with a grey stone church on the other side. As they drew closer, they could hear a chorus of enthusiastic yelling coming from a line of people standing at the edge of the field. Several boys in striped football shirts were running around in the centre of the pitch.

'There's Craig!' James pointed. 'See?'

'Oh, yes,' said Mandy, shading her eyes from the glare of the sun.

James watched keenly as the ball was smacked into the goal. Excited cheers erupted from the spectators. Mandy saw Craig dart forward and leap for the ball as it was thrown back on to the pitch from the net.

'Come on.' Mandy tugged at his sleeve. 'He'll invite you to play soon, I'm sure. Let's cross over now and head back.'

'I don't know,' James remarked, catching up with Mandy as she reached the opposite pavement. 'Craig doesn't seem terribly friendly to me.'

'He's just shy,' Mandy answered.

They strolled past a toy shop, a hairdressing salon and a chemist, and the book shop they'd seen the day before, ending up back opposite the surgery. Then Mandy spotted a display of elegant, highly polished furniture in the window next to Gibb's Groceries. 'Let's cross back,' she urged James. 'I want to look in the window of that shop.'

'Allardyce Antiques,' James read from a beautifully engraved wooden sign above the door.

'Oh, wow! Just *look* at that ornament,' Mandy cried, tugging James on to the pavement.

Just inside the window was a wide, flat area raised to the level of the window sill and carpeted in green felt. There were a number of items laid out for display on it – a decorative glass lamp and an old-fashioned chair with a pretty blue cushion – but Mandy's eyes had been drawn to a delicate porcelain carving of a cat, curled up tightly with its eyes closed. The beautiful ornament had been placed in an obliging spotlight of warm morning sunshine and its smooth china fur seemed to gleam as though it had been lighted from within.

'It's a perfect model of a Siamese cat,' Mandy said admiringly. 'Look at the dark points on its ears. I wonder how much it is?'

'I shouldn't think you could afford it,' James warned her. 'It looks a posh sort of shop to me, but it is a nice cat,' he added.

'Let's go in,' Mandy decided. 'We'll ask. I'd love to have a closer look at it anyway.'

'OK.' James shrugged. 'I could lend you a bit of my pocket money if you want.'

'Thanks,' Mandy said, reaching for the door handle.

In spite of the sunlight streaming in through the windows on either side of the door, the little shop seemed dark. Mandy blinked a couple of times to adjust her eyes and looked around. It was an

Aladdin's cave of treasure, from tiny silver pocket watches to tall wardrobes and ancient chests. Copper kettles and old pots hung from hooks on the walls.

'Now this is the sort of antique I like,' James said approvingly, reaching out for a sword in a heavy-looking brass sheath.

'Better not,' Mandy warned, edging carefully around a grandfather clock. She stood on tiptoe and craned her neck in the direction of the cat in the window. 'There doesn't seem to be anybody here... do you think it's even open?'

'I hope so,' said James.

Just then Mandy gave a gasp of surprise.

James looked around sharply. 'What?'

'It's gone!' Mandy cried. 'James, look – the ornamental cat is gone and . . . look!'

The beautiful china cat had vanished. In its place, in the exact spot where it had been lying just seconds before, there was a rather large, shaggy dog.

Three

Mandy and James stared. The dog scratched lazily at one ear, then shook its head and yawned. Tangled grey and white fur hung over its eyes and its pink tongue dripped steadily on to the green lining of the display shelf.

'But how . . . ?' James began, then stopped, frowning.

Surprised as Mandy was, she couldn't help admiring the dog. It was beautiful! It seemed to be smiling as the warmth of the sun spread through its thick, streaky coat. Mandy felt an urge to spring forward and give it a great big hug.

'Perhaps he's sitting on the cat,' James suggested.

'That wouldn't be very comfortable,' Mandy pointed out. 'More likely he's knocked it to the floor. I hope it isn't broken! Let's go over and say hello, then we'll see.'

They made their way carefully around a low, carved table holding a fine porcelain bowl.

'Do you think this dog is friendly?' James asked in a low voice. 'It might be a guard dog or something.'

'I'm sure it's friendly,' Mandy smiled. 'Look how sweet its face is! It's snoozing, that's all.'

'Can I help you?'

James and Mandy jumped, startled. Mandy spun around to see a small, round-faced man standing at the back of the shop. His cheery, interested expression put her instantly at ease. He held a pair of reading glasses in one hand.

'Are you looking for anything in particular?' he added politely.

'Hello,' said Mandy. 'We were looking at your dog, actually, and also—'

'Ah, Noodles!' The man interrupted her, shaking his head fondly as he came towards them. 'He's a character, isn't he? That little spot on the display ledge there, that's his favourite place. It gets the morning sun, you know.'

'A perfect place for sunbathing,' Mandy said.

Noodles peered up at the man through a fringe of fur. He seemed unwilling to move an inch, though Mandy could see a little stub of a tail twitching in welcome.

'He's gorgeous,' she said, reaching over the chair to pat the dog. 'Hello, Noodles.'

'He's not mine, you know,' the shop owner said unexpectedly. 'He belongs to the lady next door. He just visits – perhaps a little more often than is polite,' he added. 'I'm Thomas Allardyce, by the way.'

'I'm James Hunter,' James told him. 'This is Mandy Hope. Her parents are vets and they're looking after the MacLeod Surgery for a week.'

'Ah, yes! Welcome. You'll have a lovely time here on Jersey. Glorious weather, isn't it?'

'Yes,' Mandy agreed. She couldn't hold back a moment longer from the question she was burning to ask. 'Um, Mr Allardyce, when we were outside your shop we saw an absolutely gorgeous china cat in the window. I'm sorry to have to tell you but . . . it seems to have disappeared! It was right there, in the window and I just hope it hasn't been broken by Noodles.'

'China cat?' Mr Allardyce looked puzzled. 'An ornament, you say?'

'Yes,' Mandy said with certainty.

At that moment, a shrill little sound rang out from the back of the shop. Mandy was instantly reminded of the seagulls crying outside her window the night before. To her surprise, Mr Allardyce burst into laughter.

'An ornament!' he repeated. 'My dear, no. I think you must be referring to my beloved – and most beautiful – Ming.'

'Ming?' Mandy echoed, confused.

Mr Allardyce made a sound at the back of his throat. Instantly, a high-stepping Siamese cat with fur the colour of pearl emerged from behind a walnut cabinet and padded sedately towards them. Mandy watched, enchanted, as she wove her way delicately through the thin legs of a set of chairs, then arched her back and gave a delicate meow at Mr Allardyce's feet.

Mandy's hand flew to her mouth. 'Oh, wow!' she cried. 'You're not an ornament – you're real!'

The cat regarded them coolly through her

brilliant blue eyes. They looked to Mandy as though they had been circled with a charcoal-coloured crayon.

'She is rather a beauty,' Mr Allardyce agreed. 'Her full name is Sud Su Ming, which means "the ghost of a tiger" in Thai. I call her Ming for short.'

'How *lovely!*' Mandy bent down to scratch Ming's smooth back. The cat sank gracefully to the carpet and lay on her side, purring. 'Ghost of a tiger!'

'There's not much of the tiger about her, though,' Mr Allardyce went on. 'Noodles will insist on stealing her favourite spot in the window, and Ming is always gracious enough to let him help himself. I think she knows he's lonely, poor chap.'

'Lonely?' asked James. 'Why?' He reached down and tickled Ming under the chin. Noodles blinked at them from the window sill. He was not going to give up the spot he had snatched from Ming, though Mandy guessed he must be roasting in the sun in his furry coat.

'Oh, his owner, Mrs Gibb, is a busy lady,' Mr Allardyce explained. 'She owns the grocery shop next door,' he added.

'My dad has already been a customer there,' Mandy told him.

Ming tipped up her chin and stared at Noodles, who was puffing like a steam train. The cat's fur was as sleek as satin, her ears a deep mink colour. Each of her four paws was chocolate dark, fading to fudge brown, and then the palest cream. Mandy, who knew enough about Siamese cats to know they made friends only when they were ready, had to resist an urge to pick her up and hold her close.

'Does Ming go out at night?' she asked.

Mr Allardyce nodded. 'She's as free as a bird. Loves a bit of a wander after dark, but she's usually in her basket when I get up in the morning. Why?'

'Well,' Mandy explained, 'last night when we arrived, I heard a calling sound that I thought might be seagulls. Now that I've heard Ming, I think that she must have been making the noise.'

'That's very likely,' Mr Allardyce smiled. 'Siamese cats have a very unusual meow and they can sound just like seagulls. Some people say they sound like babies crying, too!'

'I like your pictures,' James said suddenly. Mandy saw that his attention had wandered to the wall of the shop, where Mr Allardyce had hung lots of different framed photographs, paintings and drawing of cats. James moved in closer to inspect them. 'They're fantastic,' he said.

'Thank you.' Mr Allardyce sounded pleased. 'They're not for sale. I'm mad about cats, you see, and I like collecting them for my own enjoyment.'

'They're great!' Mandy followed James over to the wall and admired the impressive collection of cat portraits. They ranged from pencil sketches of domestic pets to a spectacular white tiger caught on camera in a snowy wilderness. Some were paintings, done in bright oils; others were photographs, yellowing with age. There was even a collection of comical cat cartoons. As she stood gazing up at the display, Mandy felt Ming swirl silkily, briefly, about her bare legs. She smiled, flattered that the adorable Siamese had chosen her for this show of affection, and bent to rub her head.

Straightening up, Mandy noticed a black and white photograph of a woman smiling proudly, holding a small, frilled parasol above her head. Her long skirts were gathered in one hand, and beside her was the biggest domestic cat Mandy had ever seen. It dwarfed the trophy cup displayed at its feet.

'Gosh, *that's* an amazing cat,' Mandy said. 'The animal looked directly at the camera, its nose lifted haughtily.

'That's a Maine Coon cat,' Mr Allardyce told her. 'They're a fascinating breed. He was a champion of his class in his day, many years ago. Victorian times, that is.'

With a graceful spring, Ming landed on the padded arm-rest of a nearby chair and began a soft, contented purring. Mandy was enchanted. She cupped Ming's perfect little face in her hands, admiring the striking contrast in colour between her head and her body. Examining her closely, it seemed to Mandy that Ming looked different from other Siamese cats; she had the familiar blue eyes and chocolate points, yet her face was rounder and softer-looking than the more triangular Siamese she'd seen at Animal Ark.

James reached out to pet Ming. 'She's so beautiful,' he said. Then his face lit up as if he'd had a really good idea. 'Mandy's mum is going to be the vet on duty at a big cat show here on Friday. You could enter Ming. I'm sure she'd win.'

Mr Allardyce sat down on a wicker chair and Ming sprang on to his lap and settled herself comfortably. Her owner ran his hand over her sleek back.

'Well,' he laughed, 'it's very nice of you to say so but, you know, it isn't quite as straightforward as simply entering her.'

'What do you mean?' Mandy asked.

'Ming is an Applehead Siamese and – gorgeous though she is – I don't believe she has much of a chance competing against these modern Siamese cats.'

'I had noticed that she looks a bit different,' Mandy admitted.

'Yes,' Mr Allardyce confirmed. 'Cat breeding is subject to fashion, like everything else, and for the last few years judges and breeders have favoured a sharper, more exotic look in the breed. Wedgeheads, they're called,' he added.

'Oh,' said Mandy, disappointed. 'But that doesn't mean they're prettier or more well bred then Ming, does it?'

'I don't think so, my dear.' Mr Allardyce smiled at her. 'But there's more to a prize than just being pretty, isn't there? I mean, fashion has to be considered as well.'

'I don't understand,' said James, wrinkling his

nose. 'What's a Wedgehead? It sounds like something you'd use to prop open a door.'

Mandy and Mr Allardyce laughed.

'The standards of the show ring are constantly changing,' Mr Allardyce told them. 'Breeders these days seem to favour Wedgeheads because they are more exotic and sleeker, with larger ears and much sharper features. My Ming is curvier in appearance, as you see – rather robust, with a nice round, dark face.'

Ming looked up and narrowed her eyes at them. Then she gave a little toss of her head and began licking at her front paw. Mandy thought it was as though she were saying, 'I don't care what the standards for show cats are – I like the way I look!'

'Besides,' Mr Allardyce went on, 'I think I've got enough on my hands with the shop to run, and Ming to care for – and my pesky visitor over there.' He wagged a fond finger in Noodles' direction. The dog was still basking, though the sun had moved slightly, and he seemed unaware that he was the topic of conversation.

'He's cute,' James stated, adding rather proudly, 'I've got a dog. He's a Labrador, called Blackie.'

'A Labrador!' Thomas Allardyce looked

interested. 'I'll bet he's full of energy, like Noodles.'

'Yes, he is,' James agreed, going over to Noodles' perch to offer him some attention. 'He's lots of fun. I really like dogs – and cats, of course.'

Out of habit, James put his hand into the pocket of his jeans and groped around for the treats he usually carried for Blackie. Mandy watched him pull out a few dog biscuits, broken into bits after the long journey from Welford. At once, Noodles lifted his head, then bounded off the window sill, his eyes fixed on the goodies in James's cupped hand.

There was a splintering crash that made Mandy jump. Ming sprang off Mr Allardyce's lap in fright. Noodles had blundered straight into the oil lamp, sending it flying to the floor, where the delicate blue glass lantern shattered. James lost his footing as the dog collided with his legs. He fell in a heap on the floor and the crushed mess of biscuit flew into the air. Splintered glass lay everywhere.

'James!' Mandy cried. 'Are you all right?'

'Noodles!' Thomas Allardyce said sternly, jumping out of the chair. 'For heaven's sake, behave yourself!'

Mandy was just reaching out to give James a

hand up when a heart-rending cry made her freeze. It was a sound not unlike a baby – a very unhappy baby. Goosebumps rose on Mandy's arms. She spun around to see a pitiful sight.

'Ming!' Mandy exclaimed. 'Oh, *Ming* – what's happened to you?'

Four

Ming was behaving very strangely, so strangely that, for a moment, nobody moved. Watching the little cat tossing her head about and writhing on the carpet at first made Mandy think she was having some kind of a fit.

Her heart turned over and she and Mr Allardyce reached out for the Siamese at the same moment.

'Ming!' Mandy cried. 'Oh, Mr Allardyce, what is it?'

She tried to hold the distressed little creature, but Ming squirmed out of Mandy's grasp. Thomas Allardyce put a soothing hand on his cat's back, trying to calm her.

He withdrew his fingers quickly and put them to his nose. 'Oil!' he said, frowning. 'It's oil from that broken lamp. It's all over her, poor girl.'

'Oil?' James repeated. He had his hand looped through Noodles' collar and was struggling to hold the dog, who was still sniffing about furiously in search of biscuit crumbs. The table that Noodles had crashed into had a cracked leg and there were shards of glass everywhere. The brass base of the old-fashioned lamp lay on its side; the last drops of oil trickled on to the floor and soaked into the carpet.

Ming yowled, using first one paw then the other to wipe her face.

'I think she's got oil in her eyes,' Mandy said urgently. 'Quick! Let's take her next door to the surgery.'

'Good idea.' Mr Allardyce scooped the oily little cat into his arms and hurried off after Mandy, who had shot ahead through the maze of furniture to the door and held it open. James let go of Noodles and quickly followed.

Jennifer Locke looked up in surprise when the three of them burst through the reception door. Ming's crying alerted a small dog waiting to be seen, and it began a frantic yapping. An elderly man with a budgie in a cage at his feet covered his ears and scowled at the noise.

'Mandy!' said Jennifer. 'What on Earth has happened?'

'Is my mum with a patient, Jennifer?' Mandy asked. 'Is my dad free? Ming's covered in lamp oil and it's got into her eyes. She needs help.'

The front door opened behind them and Mandy hoped that it wasn't another emergency patient or Ming might have to wait. She turned and with relief saw that it was only Craig who had come in.

'Your father is out in the residential unit,' Jennifer said to Mandy. 'I'll get him right away.' She said hello to Craig as she slipped past him.

'Craig—' Mandy began, but she didn't finish her sentence. The half-open door to the waiting area suddenly flew open and Noodles scrambled in, his paws slipping on the linoleum floor. He made straight for James, who was standing close to Thomas Allardyce, stroking Ming.

'Hello, Noodles!' said James.

'Craig,' Mandy began again, trying unsuccessfully to grab hold of Noodles' collar. 'Can you help us? We need an extra hand to—'

'I can't,' said Craig, moving quickly through the chaos and making for the door to the stairs that led to the flat. 'I'm off out in a minute. Sorry.'

'Oh . . . OK,' said Mandy.

Noodles was leaping around all over James. His shaggy fringe bounced and his bright eyes looked merry and mischievous. 'Sit!' Mandy commanded, but Noodles took no notice.

'No more treats,' James said sternly. He showed the dog his empty hand. 'See? All gone.'

'In here, Mr Allardyce,' Jennifer called, opening the door to one of the examining rooms. 'Mr Hope will see Ming right away.'

Thomas Allardyce looked red-faced and he was out of breath as he struggled to hold Ming in his arms. She fought him, twisting and turning and rubbing her face against his jumper. She cried out again and again and the sound pierced Mandy's heart as she followed Mr Allardyce into the consulting room. What if Ming had tiny fragments of glass in her eyes?

Adam Hope immediately held out his arms to the distressed Siamese. Mr Allardyce seemed glad to hand her over.

'Thank you,' he said, flustered. 'Will you be able to get rid of the oil?'

'Oil?' Adam Hope queried, looking puzzled.

'Dad, this is Mr Allardyce from the antique shop. A lamp broke in the shop and the cat was splashed.' Mandy explained it as simply and efficiently as she could.

'Good to meet you, Mr Allardyce,' said Mr Hope, his eyes never leaving Ming. 'Poor girl,' he soothed. 'Keep still now and let me have a look at you.'

Ming sat miserably on the stainless-steel tabletop, her little body shuddering with fear. She tried to lick at the oil on her forelegs, then coughed and spat.

Adam Hope widened her eyes and looked into them with a torch. 'I can't see any damage,' he said. 'But she has oil in her eyes – paraffin, is it?'

'Yes, yes.' Thomas Allardyce nodded, looking anxious. 'A silly accident . . .'

Mandy helped her father hold Ming on the table. Outside in the waiting room, she could hear James having stern words with Noodles. Then she remembered that in their hurry to get Ming to the surgery, they'd left the door to the antique shop wide open!

'Mr Allardyce?' she said quietly. 'Would you like me to close up your shop for you?'

'The shop?' he said absently. 'Oh! *The shop* –
goodness, I've left the door open. I'd better go
back, the lock's a bit tricky. Can I leave Ming here
with you? She'll be OK now, won't she?'

'Of course,' Mandy assured him. 'We'll look
after her, don't worry.'

'Thank you so much,' said Mr Allardyce, making
hurriedly for the door.

A moment later, James appeared in the
examining room. 'He's gone,' he announced.
'The dog, I mean. Noodles. He trotted out after
Mr Allardyce. How's Ming?'

Mr Hope was just easing an injection into the
cat's upper back leg. 'I'm going to give her a
sedative,' he said. 'She's very upset; this will calm
her.'

'Dad, is she going to be all right?' Mandy asked,
her fingers caressing the only bit of fur she could
find that hadn't any oil on it. She watched as the
sedative took effect and Ming sank slowly on to the
table. Her chocolate-coloured head dropped on
to her front paws and she closed her eyes.

Adam Hope looked serious. 'Paraffin can be
absorbed through the skin,' he explained. 'It *can*
be very nasty because it can damage the liver and,

in some cases, that's fatal. But, thanks to your prompt action, we've caught this well in time.'

'What are you going to do?' asked James, his eyes as wide as saucers.

'I'm going to start by flushing out her eyes with sterile water,' Mandy's dad replied, moving around the room gathering supplies. 'Then we'll wash her very thoroughly and apply a substance that will dissolve the oil from her fur.'

'Poor Ming,' Mandy sighed. 'Cats hate water.'

'She's feeling pretty dopey,' her father reminded her. 'She won't be scared. James, could you fill the basin at the sink there with warm water for me, please? About halfway up?'

'Sure,' said James.

Once Ming's eyes had been washed, James brought over the basin of water and Mr Hope lowered the cat gently into it. Mandy held her head while her father went to work massaging the cat with a strange green jelly.

'Yuck,' said James, holding his nose. 'What a smell.'

'I agree.' Adam Hope laughed. 'But it does the trick.'

To Mandy's relief, Ming seemed unconcerned

as the smelly paste was rubbed deep into her fur. James stood at the ready with a bucket of clean water and poured it carefully over the cat's back at intervals, while Mr Hope rinsed her again and again.

When it was over, Ming looked very bedraggled and sorry for herself, but her coat was completely clean. Adam Hope wrapped her in a towel and handed her to Mandy. 'She's starting to come round now. Rub her dry, then you can take her back to Mr Allardyce,' he said. 'She doesn't need to stay in the residential unit. She's close enough for us to keep an eye on her for the next couple of days.'

'OK, thanks, Dad.' Mandy cradled the Siamese in her arms. The cat lay back like a baby, still sleepy and confused, her small face hooded in the towel. Then she opened her eyes and blinked rapidly a few times. Mandy gently stroked her with the towel to dry her off.

'Will you give Mr Allardyce these eye drops for Ming?' Adam Hope asked. 'They are protective anti-inflammatory drops. He should use them twice a day.' He handed a small bottle to James.

'Right,' James said, reading the label.

When Ming's sleek coat was smooth and shiny once more, they set off for Allardyce Antiques.

Jennifer was back behind the reception desk, working at her computer. She looked up as they went past. 'How is she?' she asked.

'Fine now,' Mandy grinned. Ming's beautiful eyes were wide open and she snuggled in closer to Mandy.

'Hey! What's this?' James said suddenly, pointing to the floor.

Mandy looked down. A thin trail of blood, scuffed by dog footprints, stained the linoleum.

'Oh!' Mandy said. 'Was the little dog that was in here earlier bleeding?'

'No,' said Jennifer, coming round from her desk to look at the floor. 'He came in for an injection.'

Mandy and James stared at each other in dismay, both clearly thinking the same thing.

'Noodles!' James cried. 'It must be Noodles. That glass . . .'

'And we never noticed!' Mandy berated herself. 'Poor Noodles!' She felt a stab of guilt. She'd been so worried about Ming, she hadn't thought to check if the big, bumbling dog had been injured too.

'Quick, Mandy,' said James, flinging open the

door and making Ming meow in surprise. 'Let's go and see if he's hurt!'

They found Thomas Allardyce in his small kitchen at the back of the shop. It was chaotically untidy, the limited countertop space crowded with papers and the small wooden table still holding the remains of Mr Allardyce's toast and marmalade. Mandy put Ming down. She immediately jumped on to a chair and began grooming herself very meticulously.

'Oh, well done!' said Mr Allardyce when he saw Ming's clean coat. 'Thank you both so much.' He gathered up the cat lovingly and she began to purr in his arms. 'She's as good as new!'

'Mr Allardyce, is Noodles with you?' asked James, looking around anxiously.

'I expect so,' he said. 'Yes, there he is. Over there – for some reason the silly dog has squeezed himself right under that chair.'

'We think he's hurt,' Mandy told him. 'There's blood on the floor in the surgery.'

'Oh, dear,' said Mr Allardyce, frowning.

James and Mandy went over to where Noodles was lying under a low padded chair, licking repeatedly at an upturned front paw.

'It's cut all right,' James said grimly. 'It looks sore.'

'Oh, poor Noodles!' Mandy squatted to peer under the armchair.

Noodles wouldn't let Mandy touch his paw but she could see that it would need stitching. The glass had sliced quite deeply into the soft, rounded part of the pad.

'This is all my fault,' said James. 'If I hadn't offered Noodles a treat, none of this would have happened.'

'Don't blame yourself,' Mandy told him. 'It was an accident, that's all.'

James nodded gloomily and Thomas Allardyce put a kind hand on his shoulder.

'Just bad luck, lad,' he said. 'Look, would you two be kind and take Noodles to the surgery to have his paw looked at? I'll see if I can get hold of Mrs Gibb, his owner. She ought to know.'

'Yes, of course, Mr Allardyce,' Mandy said.

'Thank you both so much,' he replied. Looking at his cat, he smiled gratefully. Ming lay contentedly in his arms now, looking around her with interest, like a queen on a throne.

'Come on,' said Mandy. 'Let's get patient number two next door!'

It was late in the afternoon by the time Noodles' small operation was over. Mr and Mrs Hope had been busy, and, because the dog's cut paw hadn't been considered urgent, they'd had to wait. Noodles seemed subdued as he sat in the waiting room. James held him tightly on a lead that he'd found in the residential unit, but the dog was too busy licking at his sore foot to be any trouble. Around one o'clock, Jennifer brought in a plate of sandwiches for Mandy and James and Noodles showed only mild interest. His nose twitched and he sniffed loudly but didn't get up to investigate the source of the delicious smell. Finally, he emerged from the treatment room with four neat stitches and a solid bandage around his leg.

'Noodles!' James crouched down and hugged the dog. 'I'm sorry, boy.'

'The stitches will dissolve in time, Mandy. Will you tell that to Mrs Gibb, please? She won't have to bring him back to have them removed.'

'OK, Dad,' Mandy replied, smoothing Noodles' shaggy head with the palm of her hand. 'Good boy,' she told him and clipped a lead to his collar.

James and Mandy walked him slowly, gingerly back to Gibb's Groceries. A sign in the window read closed so they went next door to Mr Allardyce's shop. Opening the door, Mandy saw he had a customer, a middle-aged woman with blonde hair.

'Ah! Here he is now!' Mr Allardyce had spotted them at the door.

'Noodles!' The woman hurried over and stooped to give the dog a cuddle. 'What have you been up to now?'

'Sarah Jane,' Thomas Allardyce said, 'this is Mandy and James, the pair I was telling you about.

Mrs Gibb has just come back from a trip to the other side of the island so she's only just heard about the accident.'

'Hello,' James and Mandy said together.

'Thank you, thank you,' Mrs Gibb said gratefully. 'You've been a wonderful help.'

'Well,' James began, looking guilty. 'I haven't been really . . .' before Mandy stopped him with a nudge.

'We're glad to have helped,' she smiled.

'There was a small piece of glass in Noodles' paw,' James reported. 'Mr Hope dug it out and he's going to be fine. He has a few stitches.'

'Dissolving ones,' Mandy added. 'You won't have to take him back, my dad said.'

'I'm very grateful,' said Mrs Gibb. She pushed back the dog's thick fringe with her hand and looked into his eyes. 'What am I going to do with you?' she sighed.

'To be honest, Sarah Jane,' Thomas Allardyce spoke up, 'he's becoming a bit of a nuisance in the shop. He's just too boisterous to be jumping about in here! It's not the damage to the lamp or anything that I'm worried about, but I'd hate to see him get hurt again.'

'I know.' Mrs Gibb shook her head sadly. 'I expect it's because he's bored. He loves to get out, but, really, I haven't the time to walk him.'

'Could we help?' Mandy offered automatically. She was sure they'd be able to fit a little dog-sitting around their chores in the surgery.

'Yes!' James sounded very enthusiastic. Mandy guessed he wanted to make amends for the accident.

'Well,' Sarah Jane said, 'that would be very kind. Noodles would adore to get out a bit more. He hasn't had many really good, long walks since my son left for university on the mainland.'

There was a tap at the door and Emily and Adam Hope came in. Mandy did the introductions.

'Surgery's closed for the day,' Adam Hope said. 'We just came by to check on these two.'

All eyes turned to Ming and Noodles. Ming was making her way delicately across the floor to the spot in the window she loved. She paused to lick at a patch of damp coat, then jumped up and glared pointedly at her rival, who was still sitting by Mrs Gibb. Noodles was watching her with his head cocked to one side and his ears pricked. For a second, it looked to Mandy as though the dog was going to challenge Ming for the best sunbathing spot. He started forward, then seemed to think better of it. He lifted his sore leg and looked at James with a mournful expression on his face. Then he sighed and lay down instead with his head on James's foot. Ming curled up in the window for a nap.

'Ming has reclaimed her territory!' Mandy declared. 'Good for her. I guess getting oil on her fur was the last straw!'

Five

Mid-morning on Sunday, they all drove out to the Sullivans' farm listed in the appointment book. It had dawned cool and cloudy after overnight rain, but Mandy thought it made the island look even more beautiful. The sea seemed restless; it was pearly grey rather than blue and the low clouds only made the strong summer colours below more intense.

Mandy sat in the back of the MacLeods' Land-rover looking eagerly around her. Outside Beaumont, the trees lining the narrow roads met overhead, making a tunnel of soft green light.

'Do you think Mrs Sullivan will mind us coming along?' she asked her father.

'I shouldn't think so,' he replied, adding teasingly, 'unless you intend to kidnap one of her calves!'

Mandy laughed and passed James a tube of peppermints.

'I like the way cows *smell*,' James remarked, his cheek bulging with the mint. 'They remind me of the way a meadow smells.'

On Mandy's side, a field of buttercups spread away down to the sea. A group of young heifer cows looked up from their grazing to stare curiously as the Land-rover passed. It was such a gorgeous place! Mandy wondered what it would be like to live on the island all the time and that made her think about Craig.

'What's Craig doing today?' she asked out loud.

Mrs Hope turned and held out her hand for a mint. 'I'm not sure, but he seemed happy enough to stay behind. Football's been cancelled because of the rain. The pitch is wet, he told me.'

'He should have come along with us!' James said generously.

'Yes,' Mandy agreed.

'I offered,' said Emily Hope. 'He didn't seem too keen.'

'He's still shy of us,' Mandy concluded. 'It's a shame.'

'He must feel awkward, having us in his home,' said Mr Hope. 'He's just a private sort of person, I think.'

'I know,' said James. 'We could ask him if he wants to walk Noodles with us later.'

Mrs Hope smiled at him. 'That's a good idea. But don't take it personally if he says no. If he wants to get involved with us, he'll let us know.'

Mandy sighed. 'It's a shame,' she said again. She couldn't understand Craig. He had the long summer holidays stretching before him – and could see all the wonderful animals that came and went from his parents' surgery. Yet he didn't seem a bit excited about any of that.

'Look, James,' said Mrs Hope, pointing. 'Yet another place serving cream teas!'

'Oh, yum!' James rubbed his tummy dramatically.

'Honestly,' Mandy teased, holding the peppermints away from James's reaching hand, 'at this rate you're going to explode before we get back to Welford!'

'Here we are,' said Adam Hope. 'Misty Hills Farm.'

White fenceposts surrounded a few acres of lush green paddocks at the side of the road.

'Gosh,' Mandy said. 'It looks lovely.'

Adam Hope pulled into the gravel driveway and drove slowly towards the big, thatched house. In the centre of a circular parking area, there was a small island of plants. The noise from the engine startled a skinny, light-brown cat, which shot out from under a bush and leapt up the nearest tree.

'That,' said Emily Hope, getting out of the car and wagging a finger in the direction of the vanishing cat, 'is a Cornish Rex.'

'Oh, well done, Mum!' Mandy said approvingly. 'You can spot these breeds at a hundred paces after all the reading you've done.'

'I don't want to be caught out by any technical questions from the breeders at the show,' her mother replied, giving her a wry smile.

'Good morning!' A woman in wellington boots was striding towards them. 'You must be standing in for Colin and Anna. I'm Aline Sullivan. Thanks for coming out.'

Mr and Mrs Hope shook her hand and introduced James and Mandy.

'You must be keen,' Mrs Sullivan said with a smile, 'coming out to a farm on a Sunday morning just to see some stitches being taken out.'

'We are,' Mandy replied. 'We'd love to see the animals, if you don't mind.'

'I don't mind a bit.' She turned to Mandy's parents. 'Would you take a look at one of my calves while you're here?'

'Gladly,' said Mr Hope, lifting his big black veterinary bag.

'We enjoyed the drive here,' said Emily Hope, falling into step beside the farmer. 'We haven't had much time to drive around.'

'Well, I shan't keep you too long from exploring further,' said Mrs Sullivan. 'This way!'

They followed the farmer to the milking parlour. Treading carefully in the ooze of mud along the path, Mandy spotted a large herd of pale brown cows in the adjacent pasture. They pulled at the grass, flicking their tails to keep the flies away. One or two of the more curious animals ambled up to the fence.

'Aren't you lovely!' Mandy said.

Beside her, James was breathing in rather loudly. Mandy tweaked his T-shirt.

'I told you,' James grumbled. 'I like the smell!'

Mandy feasted her eyes on the animals' beautiful faces. Huge, liquid-brown eyes gazed at her with interest, and they blinked long lashes and lifted their wet grey noses to sniff at her hands.

Mrs Sullivan took them to a calving pen. Three calves lay dozing in the straw. When Mrs Sullivan led the Hopes in, two of them clambered to their feet in alarm. The tiniest calf remained where it was.

'This is our little Katie,' explained Mrs Sullivan, crouching down beside her. 'She was born small, five weeks ago. She's been off her food recently . . .' She trailed off, looking up at Mr and Mrs Hope.

James and Mandy squeezed up to the railing. Mandy wanted to be as close to the little calf as possible without getting in the way. Katie stared at them with big, bewildered eyes. Then she stood up nervously on her wobbly legs. Mandy wanted to reach out to her, but she knew better. The calf was sick, she could see that. Katie was struggling to breathe and her nose was running.

'My bet is that she has a respiratory infection,' Adam Hope said right away, delving into his

black bag for a thermometer. 'I'll just take her temperature.'

The calf skittered away from Mr Hope as he approached. Mrs Sullivan slipped her arms around Katie's neck, holding her still and talking to her in a soothing tone.

'Yes, her temperature is up,' Mr Hope said, after a moment. 'I'll give her an antibiotic injection, and also an anti-inflammatory shot. That should clear things up.'

'She'll be much better soon,' Mrs Hope assured the farmer. 'But give us a ring if she doesn't start eating normally within the next couple of days.'

Mandy watched her father as he filled his syringe and inserted the needle quickly into the big muscle on the calf's back, near her tail. Katie shifted, alarmed, but it was all over in seconds.

'Poor Katie,' Mandy said quietly.

'It's a fairly common infection in calves,' her mother told her. 'We've caught it in time so it won't turn to pneumonia, that's the main thing.'

'Good,' said James, stretching an arm through the railing to risk a gentle stroke. Katie didn't move, so Mandy put out her hand and touched the calf's velvety ear.

'Oh, she's amazing,' she breathed.

'I expect you've worked up an appetite?' Aline Sullivan asked, opening the gate of the pen. 'I hope so, because we use our own dairy cream to make the most scrumptious cream teas.'

'Wow!' James's eyebrows shot up. 'Really? Here?'

'Right here, up at the back of the house. Do you fancy a scone?'

'I'll say!' James grinned.

'Sounds good to me,' agreed Mrs Hope.

'Excellent,' Adam Hope agreed. 'I'll join you after I've removed those stitches, shall I?'

'Ah, yes, that'll be Doris. She's outside in the field. I'll take you to her,' Mrs Sullivan said.

'Don't eat all the scones, James!' Mr Hope warned. 'I'll be back in a few minutes.'

Mandy laughed as she went out into the yard, squinting in the bright sunshine.

Mrs Hope caught up with her. 'Well,' she said, '*are* they any different to the Jersey cows we have at home?'

'Yes,' Mandy insisted. 'I think they are. Somehow, they seem to belong here – much more than they do out on the moor.'

Emily Hope slipped an arm around Mandy's shoulders and gave her a quick hug. 'And now we're about to sample Jersey cream from Jersey cows on Jersey,' she said. 'What could be better?'

Ten minutes later, when they had washed their hands in the kitchen, Mrs Sullivan served them all the promised cream tea. Mr Hope carried the tray to a wooden table outside and James sprang up to help unload a plate piled high with delicious-looking scones. There was a pot of strawberry jam and a bowl brimming with thick, yellowish cream.

'Hmm,' said Emily Hope. 'What a bonus! Thank you.'

Mandy poured juice for herself and James; for the adults, there was tea. James sliced his fluffy scone in two and lathered it deeply with cream, then added a generous dollop of jam.

'Fantastic,' he said, smiling at Mrs Sullivan.

'I'm glad you like it,' she answered.

When neither James nor Mandy could eat another mouthful, they asked if they could go and have a look around the farm. Mrs Sullivan readily agreed and topped up the teacups for Mr and Mrs Hope.

They walked to the field where the Jersey herd was grazing. Mandy climbed astride the split pole fence. The sun had come out and several cows lay basking, chewing the cud.

A few of the smaller, younger cows were walking towards the fence. As they came nearer, the nervous little heifers drew up short of the barrier, stretching their necks to investigate the hands of the strangers from a safe distance. By keeping very still, Mandy attracted a curious calf that came close enough to snuffle the palm of her hand.

All too soon, Mandy heard her mother calling.

'Time to go!' Emily Hope waved at them from the other side of the field. When Mandy jumped down from the fence, the cows scattered in all directions.

Walking back towards the Land-rover, James spotted the cat Mrs Hope had named as a Cornish Rex. It had found an upturned milk crate to sit on and was grooming itself with its eyes closed.

'Only a few more days to the show,' Mandy remembered. 'It's going to be such fun.'

'Yes,' James agreed. 'It's a shame that Ming won't be taking part though, especially now that her coat is so clean!'

Then, as Adam Hope jangled the car keys loudly to urge them to hurry, he and Mandy broke into a run.

When they arrived at the surgery, Craig was in the back garden kicking a football around. He raised a hand in silent greeting, then went back to aiming at the goal.

James bent down by the back door to take off his muddy trainers. Suddenly, the side gate opened and Noodles burst in and fell upon James with glee.

'Noodles!' cried Mrs Gibb, who was dragged in

behind her dog. 'Do *stop* it!' She tugged hard at his lead. 'I was just coming to ask if you'd mind giving him a walk before lunch, Mandy?' she added, as James hopped around trying to retrieve one of his shoes.

'Yes, we'd love to,' Mandy smiled, trying hard not to laugh at poor James. Noodles obviously adored him.

'Oh, good,' Mrs Gibb said. 'How kind of you.'

She closed the side gate behind her and unclipped the dog's lead. Noodles bounded around; every bit of him seemed to be trembling with excitement. Suddenly he spotted the ball – and Craig. He went lumbering over, his large pink tongue lolling.

For a moment, Mandy hoped the friendly dog might encourage Craig to join them on a walk. But it had the opposite effect. She stared in amazement as Craig snatched up his football and tucked it firmly under one arm. Then, giving Noodles a wide berth, he marched briskly across the lawn and, his eyes fixed on the ground, slipped in through the side door of the house. The door closed with a slam behind him.

Six

There was no time to wonder about Craig's bad temper. Noodles quickly turned his attention to Mandy. He ran over, jumped up and put his two big front paws on her shoulders, barking joyfully.

'He's such a handful,' said Sarah Jane Gibb, shushing the dog with a wave of her hand and giving Mandy the lead. 'Do you think you'll manage?'

Mandy grinned as she eased Noodles down to the ground. 'Oh, we're used to dogs that are a handful,' she said.

James was barefoot, brushing off the dirt from

the farm that had got in between his toes. 'He can't be bouncier than Blackie!' he agreed, grimacing.

'You'd better put your shoes back on,' Mandy told him. 'Noodles is ready to go right now.'

As James pushed his feet into his trainers, Mrs Hope rapped on the kitchen window to attract their attention.

'Would you two like a drink?' she asked, opening the window and looking out at them.

'We're going to take Noodles for a walk,' Mandy explained. 'Is that OK?'

'Fine,' she said. 'See you later. Have fun.'

Mandy had secured Noodles by a short lead. Now, she handed it to James. 'You can take him first, since he likes you so much!' she smiled.

James was immediately tugged in the direction of the garden gate. Noodles seemed to know exactly where he was going.

Mandy caught up with them, laughing. 'It's just like being at home with Blackie,' she said.

The sky had been washed to a beautiful blue by the rain. Mandy had a spring in her step as she walked briskly beside James, who was trying to keep Noodles in check. The dog coughed, and James hurriedly slackened the lead. They'd turned

left out of the surgery car park and headed along
the main street. Mandy spotted Mr Allardyce
outside his shop, and she waved.

'I wish I could let Noodles off the lead,' said
James. 'He'd like a good run, in spite of his sore leg.'

'He's only limping slightly,' Mandy said. 'And if
this walk goes well, maybe Mrs Gibb will let us take
Noodles to the beach tomorrow.'

Noodles, it seemed, was well known around
Beaumont. Several people reached down to pat
him on the head as they passed and some asked
about his bandaged paw. One woman with dark
curly hair stopped to offer him a biscuit from the
basket she was carrying.

'I know you,' she said, stooping and rubbing the
dog on the head, 'but I don't know who *you* are!'
She smiled at Mandy and James.

Mandy smiled back. 'I'm Mandy Hope and this
is my friend James Hunter. We're staying at the
MacLeods' veterinary surgery.'

'We offered to give Noodles a walk,' James
explained.

'Sarah Jane will be pleased!' said the woman. 'Is
his paw mending?' Mandy and James had squeezed
to the side of the narrow pavement to allow people

to pass. But Noodles was impatient to be off, and kept pulling on the lead and coughing loudly. They were attracting quite a few looks.

'Yes,' Mandy laughed. 'It doesn't seem to have slowed him down one bit!'

'Oh dear,' the woman said. 'We're making nuisances of ourselves. Look, I'll tell you what. I've got a big garden with lots of lawn. Would you like to bring Noodles along for a change of scene? I understand he might not be able to run in the park until his paw is better.'

'Well…' Mandy began hesitantly.

'I'm Deborah Stewart,' the woman introduced herself. 'I know the MacLeods and Sarah Jane Gibb – and I only live a few doors down at number eighteen.' She pointed along the street.

'OK, thank you,' Mandy said.

Mrs Stewart stepped briskly ahead, her basket swinging. Mandy and James followed.

While they walked the short distance to number eighteen, Mandy explained to Mrs Stewart that both her parents were vets.

'Ah,' she said. 'I know something about your mother! Isn't she going to be the on-site vet at the cat show here on Saturday?'

'Yes,' Mandy said, feeling rather proud. Her mother was famous already!

'The whole village is looking forward to the show,' Mrs Stewart went on. 'We've got visitors coming from all over the world – even as far as Japan!'

'Wow,' James breathed, as Mandy felt a small pang of excitement.

'Here we are,' said Mrs Stewart, fishing in her basket for a door key in front of a whitewashed cottage with a slate roof.

Mandy guessed that she was a keen gardener because there were earthenware pots brimming with exotic flowering plants everywhere. She looked around her nervously. 'Are you sure Noodles is safe in your garden? I'd hate it if he broke anything.'

'He'll be fine,' said Mrs Stewart, leading them indoors. 'All he wants is space to tear around and let off a bit of steam. Here we are, James.' She opened a glass door to a lovely garden. 'Let him rip! I'll get you both a cold drink. You look as if you deserve one!'

Noodles was giving off little yelps of joy as James undid the clasp and let him go, the dog's paws scrabbling against the polished floorboards in his eagerness to explore. He shot out of the door and tore off across a smooth green lawn surrounded by a blaze of colourful flowers.

Mandy and James watched him for a moment, then Mandy went into the kitchen to help Mrs Stewart. On the way through the sitting room, she noticed a cat curled up in a smooth little ball in the centre of a deep, puffy cushion. One chocolate paw lay loosely over its face and a gentle rumble came from the cat as it snoozed.

Mandy stopped. 'A Siamese!' she said aloud, just as Mrs Stewart appeared with a tray.

'Do you like cats?' She smiled. 'I adore them. This one is my pride and joy. Supreme Champion – Black Forest Gateau.'

Mandy gaped at the cat, then at Mrs Stewart. 'Is that really his name?'

'Yes,' she answered, setting down the tray on a coffee table in front of the sofa. 'Just Gateau for short. It means "cake" in French, you know. Very fitting – he's chocolate in colour and certainly sweet enough!'

Mandy laughed and pointed out the sleeping cat to James as he joined them.

'Oh, wow,' he said, his hands on his hips. 'Another one!'

'You have a Siamese, do you?' Mrs Stewart looked very interested. She paused as she was pouring cola into two glasses.

'No,' James shook his head. 'I don't. But we met one.'

'Ming,' Mandy explained. 'She belongs to Mr Allardyce.'

'Ah, Ming!' Deborah Stewart smiled. 'Yes, I know Thomas's lovely Ming quite well. She's an Applehead Siamese, like Gateau.'

As though he knew he was being talked about, the cat slowly uncurled and opened first one eye, then the other. He stretched lazily, then jumped off the sofa and ran across to his owner, calling out a noisy greeting.

Mrs Stewart gathered the cat into her arms and kissed his face before setting him down in her lap. Settling against her, Gateau put out a languid front paw and gently batted at the earring dangling from Mrs Stewart's ear.

'Oh no, you don't, you mischievous old man,' she chided him, laughing. 'He's full of tricks, in spite of his age.'

Gateau soaked up the attentions of the two visitors, purring as they stroked and petted him. His magnificent chocolate paws kneaded the soft wool of his owner's lilac jumper.

'He *looks* like a champion!' Mandy said, admiring the almost black face of the cat.

'Oh, yes,' said Mrs Stewart. 'He's a champ all right. He's won the Gold Challenge Certificate three times. He's retired now, of course.'

'Did he like it?' asked James.

'Being shown?' Mrs Stewart was tickling her cat under his chin. 'He loved the attention he got,' she replied. 'As I'm sure you know, Siamese are very sociable animals and make wonderful pets. They're affectionate, fun and highly intelligent – not to mention gorgeous to look at!'

Gateau raised his chin, looking his most imperious, and everybody laughed.

'Cat shows have an important role to play,' Mrs Stewart went on. 'Careful selection of the very finest cats helps keep the breed strong because the cats pass on those strengths to future generations.'

'I think the Appleheads are beautiful!' Mandy declared. 'But Mr Allardyce told us that they aren't as popular at shows now.'

'Well, Appleheads are one of the oldest breeds of domestic cat in the world. They look much the same as when the breed was originally imported from Siam – a muscular, athletic cat with a round head and brilliant blue eyes.' Mandy noticed a fleeting shadow of sadness cross Deborah Stewart's face. 'I hope they don't die out altogether as a breed.'

Mandy was thinking about this when she heard James splutter and gasp. She looked across at him, surprised. His face was a picture of shock. He was kneeling at the foot of Mrs Stewart's armchair, staring straight ahead, his fingers frozen in Gateau's soft fur. For a moment, Mandy thought he might be choking – he seemed unable to speak – then a sudden movement made her look down at James's bare legs. A large, brightly coloured snake had entwined itself around his left thigh.

'Oh!' said Mandy, startled.

Just then, the door flew open and a tall, dark-haired young woman rushed into the room.

'Mum, have you seen Kellogg?' she said, sounding exasperated. 'I've looked . . . oh, hello, sorry to interrupt.'

'Kellogg?' James squeaked.

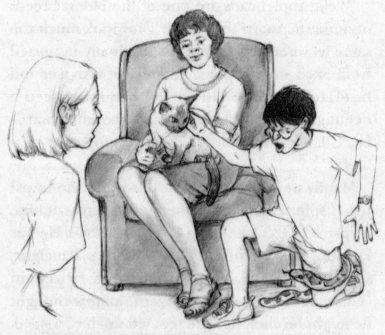

'Is Kellogg a snake, by any chance?' Mandy asked.

'That would be my Kellogg,' the girl said cheerfully.

'Right . . . there,' Mandy pointed slowly, wondering if any sudden movement in James's direction might alarm the creature.

'Oh, *there* you are!' said the girl, striding towards James.

'Does he bite?' James wanted to know, in a very small voice.

Mrs Stewart peered down at the snake in surprise. 'Goodness, Kellogg! The places you turn up! He's a harmless little fellow, James, even if he should have been called Houdini! Nicole, this is Mandy and James. They're staying at the MacLeods' and Mandy's mum's going to be the vet at the show.'

'Hi!' Nicole responded, stooping to unwind the snake from James's leg. It was over half a metre long, with wide, orange stripes edged in black. 'Sorry about that. He must have been under the chair and taken a fancy to the warmth he could sense around him – and that was you!'

'Oh,' said James, relief spreading across his face as the snake was uncoiled and removed. 'I just got a surprise.'

'I'm sure you did!' Nicole laughed, her dark brown curls jiggling. 'Don't worry about Kellogg. He's a corn snake. I've had him ages and he's a great friend.'

Mandy couldn't help feeling sorry for James, who had gone quite pale. He took a sip of his cola just as Noodles began scraping loudly and persistently at the door from outside.

'Can I let him in?' asked James, glancing at Kellogg.

'I'll take Kellogg to his vivarium,' said Nicole. 'He's off his food at the moment and I'm trying to encourage him to eat.'

James hurried to let Noodles in. The dog was panting from his run around the garden. His stumped tail wagged hard as he went around the room greeting everybody in turn. Then, to Mandy and James's surprise, he flopped down at James's feet and gave a great sigh of contentment.

'That run certainly did him a lot of good,' Mrs Stewart commented. 'It's lovely to see Noodles behaving calmly. You must be a good influence, you two!'

Nicole had draped Kellogg around her neck like a scarf, and the snake seemed quite happy. His head bobbed about and Mandy watched, fascinated, as he suddenly disappeared down the back of Nicole's T-shirt.

'How was work this morning?' her mother asked her.

Nicole pulled a face. 'We're so busy!' she said, wriggling her shoulders as Kellogg reappeared at her neck. 'We're expecting this huge crowd of visitors to be staying at the hotel because of the cat show and there's so much to do before we're ready.'

'Nicole works at the Bay Hotel,' Mrs Stewart explained, stroking Gateau. To Mandy's amazement, the elderly Siamese looked completely untroubled by the appearance of the snake and the dog.

'I'm still trying to think up an idea for a theme for the weekend, something that will unite all the cat lovers,' Nicole filled them in. 'I thought it would make a nice welcome.'

'Is there going to be a celebration dinner or something?' Mandy asked, interested.

'No, more like a display in the foyer of the hotel . . . I don't know . . . I just haven't settled on anything suitable yet.' Nicole sighed. 'Perhaps it's not such a good idea after all.'

'You haven't much time left to get it done,' Mrs Stewart reminded her.

Nicole groaned. 'Don't I know it!'

Kellogg dabbed gently at his owner's face as she spoke, and James began to giggle. Only the lower half of the girl's face was visible – she looked to Mandy as though she were wearing an exotic hat.

'Enough!' Nicole laughed, standing up, 'I think Kellogg is trying to tell me something. He might even be hungry at last, with any luck. It was nice to meet you both.'

'Bye,' Mandy said. 'Good luck with finding your theme for the hotel.'

'Thanks, bye.'

Gateau stood up and stretched luxuriously in Mrs Stewart's lap. Mandy thought again how beautiful he was. 'Mrs Stewart,' she asked, 'do you think there will be any Applehead Siamese entered in this year's show?' Now that she'd met these two glorious specimens, she was keen to see some more.

'I'm not certain, Mandy,' replied Mrs Stewart. 'I don't know anybody that has registered an Applehead for entry around here.'

'What about Gateau?' James suggested.

'He's way past it now, I'm afraid,' Mrs Stewart chuckled.

'Well, what about Ming?' Mandy piped up.

'Ming?' Mrs Stewart raised her eyebrows. 'Well, Ming, of course, is a beauty, but Thomas Allardyce won't be persuaded to enter her. At least, I don't think he will.'

'Do you think she has a chance of winning?' Mandy persisted.

'I should think so, yes,' Mrs Stewart nodded. 'It would be wonderful but, knowing Thomas as I do, I really don't think he'd be interested.'

Mandy stood up. 'I think people should be reminded how Siamese used to look. Wedgeheads are beautiful, but Appleheads deserve equal recognition.'

Mrs Stewart smiled. 'I'm sure Thomas would agree with you, but . . .' She raised her hands, palms up, and shrugged.

'Let's go and talk to him,' said James. 'I'll bet he'll listen to us.'

'It's time we went back anyway,' Mandy said. 'Thanks for having us, Mrs Stewart.

'It's been lovely to meet you,' she said. 'And nice to see Noodles so placid for a change!'

Noodles stood up obediently and James clipped on his lead. At once, the dog began to tug James gently towards the door, as though he expected another adventure.

'What time is it?' Mandy asked James, as they waved goodbye to Mrs Stewart.

James grinned. 'Mr Allardyce's shop is still open, if that's what you mean!'

'Right,' said Mandy. 'Come on! We've got some persuading to do!'

Seven

They found Mr Allardyce polishing a copper vase. When the door opened, he looked up and removed his glasses.

'Hello there.' He smiled. Standing, he put out a hand to keep a bouncing Noodles at bay. 'No you don't, my friend.'

James tugged a little harder to keep the dog in check.

'Hello, Mr Allardyce,' Mandy said. 'How's Ming?'

'Almost as good as new!' he replied. 'She went out for a prowl last evening as if nothing had happened.'

'Good!' Mandy and James said together.

Mr Allardyce glanced at his wristwatch. 'I was just thinking of closing up. Is there something I can do for you?' he said kindly. 'Or have you come to visit Ming?'

Mandy smiled. 'Well, we wanted to *talk* to you about Ming. Are you in a hurry to leave?'

'Never in a hurry to leave the company of good friends,' said Mr Allardyce, his eyes twinkling. 'Pull up a chair, both of you. This sounds like business to me.'

'Can I let Noodles wander?' James asked. 'He's been running around all morning so I expect he's feeling less boisterous.'

'In that case, yes. I expect he'll go and nose out poor Ming – but we're used to that!'

Mandy couldn't wait to tell Mr Allardyce about the idea that had been simmering in her mind ever since she'd spoken to Mrs Stewart. She clasped her hands on her knees and looked seriously at him.

'We have come to ask you if you would enter Ming for the cat show on Saturday,' she began. 'You see, we think she might enjoy it, and other people would love to see her, I'm sure.'

'How kind you are to think of her!' Mr Allardyce smiled, looking every inch a proud father. 'But, you see, it's not that I'm not in *favour* of cat shows, it's just that it would mean closing my shop for a whole day. Also, she'll need grooming and—'

'We could groom her!' James put in.

'I could mind the shop for you!' Mandy added.

'No.' James shook his head. 'That wouldn't work. You've got to be at the show to help your mum, remember?'

'Oh, yes.' Mandy frowned.

'May I ask *why* you're so keen for Ming to compete?' asked Mr Allardyce, looking from Mandy to James and back again.

'She's so beautiful!' Mandy blurted out. 'She would perfectly represent the breed – her breed – at an important show. After all, Appleheads are an ancient, traditional breed.'

'That's right,' said James. 'It's really important.'

'Sounds like you've been having a chat with the experts!' Mr Allardyce chuckled.

'We've been talking to Mrs Stewart,' Mandy confessed. 'She told us that she used to show Gateau, but he's too old now. She thought Ming would be a great candidate.'

'But do you really think she has much of a chance against the Wedgeheads?' Mr Allardyce wondered.

'Yes!' Mandy said with determination. 'Anyway, the main thing isn't winning but showing people that there are other, more traditional types of Siamese. We don't need a judge to tell us that Ming is the most beautiful cat on the island!'

'Well . . .' Mr Allardyce was silent for a moment, thinking. Then he slapped his hand on his knee in triumph. 'I've got an idea. Why don't you enter her for the show? I'll entrust Ming to your good care. You can prepare her for the show and enter her yourselves. You'll still have time to help your mum. How about that?'

'Really?' Mandy's eyes were wide. 'That would be great!'

'We'll make you proud,' James promised. 'She'll be the best-looking cat there.'

Thomas Allardyce laughed. 'There we are then, that's settled. Just tell me what you need to do for the entry.'

'Thanks, Mr Allardyce.' Mandy jumped up. 'I'll check with Mum and let you know.'

James went over to collect Noodles who had discovered a few remaining crumbs from the dog treats James had spilled and was enthusiastically licking the carpet.

'Come on, boy,' he said. 'We'd better get you back to Mrs Gibb.' He clipped on Noodles' lead once more.

'Goodbye for now,' Mandy said to Mr Allardyce. 'We'll let you know what needs to be done.'

'Good,' said Mr Allardyce, patting Noodles. 'After all, there isn't much time now, is there?' And to Mandy's delight, he looked almost as excited as she was about the prospect of entering Ming in the show.

Mandy had hoped to have her mother's full attention when they reached the surgery, but as soon as they entered the waiting room, she knew she was going to be disappointed. Nicole Stewart had just arrived with Kellogg in a cloth bag. She looked worried.

'A corn snake!' Mandy's mother was saying, as Mandy and James put their heads around the open door to one of the consulting rooms. Kellogg raised his head and blinked at her, swaying lightly from side to side. 'Isn't he handsome?'

'Isn't he?' Nicole agreed, smiling a greeting at James and Mandy. 'But he hasn't eaten anything for days. When he refused food again today, I thought I had better bring him in. I'm sorry to have come on a Sunday, but I am really worried.'

'It's no problem. We were only going to have a sandwich for lunch so it can wait. Let's take a look at you,' Emily Hope said, gently lifting the snake out of the bag. James stood well back from the examining table while Kellogg's eyes were examined and Mandy guessed he was still feeling wary after his dramatic introduction to the snake.

'His eyes are cloudy, which means he's about to shed his beautiful skin,' said Emily Hope, 'but I can't see any mites in either eye, so that's good.' She ran her hand slowly down the length of the snake's body, feeling for any swellings. Then she opened Kellogg's mouth by pressing softly on either side of his jaw. Mandy watched, fascinated. They very rarely treated reptiles in Welford and she knew she'd have to learn lots about them when she trained to be a vet.

Shining a small torch inside the gaping pink cavity, Mrs Hope saw what she needed to make a diagnosis. 'Oh, I can see what the problem is,' she said. 'His tongue is pale rather than a healthy red. I think he has an infection in his mouth – *infectious stomatis*, it's called.'

'Gosh,' Mandy said. 'That sounds serious.'

'Can it be treated?' Nicole asked anxiously.

'Very simply,' said Emily Hope. 'I'll give you a course of antibiotic drops. It should clear up quite quickly, then he'll get his appetite back!'

'Thank you.' Nicole smiled gratefully. She opened the cloth bag and Kellogg slithered into it, eagerly seeking the familiar dark. 'Poor Kellogg. I'm not surprised he hasn't wanted to eat if his mouth's been so sore.'

Mandy and James followed Nicole out into the waiting room while Mrs Hope went to the store-room to get the drops. Jennifer smiled at them briefly, then went back to her computer. She had come into work to catch up on some ordering while the surgery was officially closed.

'Have you come up with any ideas yet? For your hotel theme, I mean?' James asked Nicole.

The young woman shook her head. 'No, I'm still hoping for inspiration,' she admitted.

'Here we are.' Emily Hope held out a small bottle but as Nicole reached to take it, Kellogg's bag slipped from her grasp. The snake fell to the floor with a dull little thud.

'Kellogg!' Nicole gasped, as her pet poked his

head out of the opening and began gliding rapidly towards the cover of the reception desk. At that moment, Craig came into the room.

'Grab him!' Mandy yelled, lunging for Kellogg before he vanished under the desk. The corn snake slithered out of reach.

James got down on his knees beside Nicole, while Mrs Hope dashed around to the other side of the desk in an attempt to head Kellogg back out into the open. Mandy glanced up at Craig, and she was so surprised by the expression on his face that, for a second, she couldn't move.

Craig had gone chalk white. His eyes bulged and his mouth hung open. His back was pressed up against the door to the hall, his fingers splayed against the white wood behind him. Without taking his eyes from the floor, he tried to take a step backward, then realised the door was shut. Mandy saw he was breathing very fast. He squeezed his eyes tight shut for a second, then opened them and sprinted across the room and out of the front door to the street. It was all over in a trice – and nobody except Mandy seemed to have noticed!

Mrs Hope gave a triumphant cry. 'Got you!'

Mandy turned her attention back to Kellogg and

watched as the end of his marked tail disappeared back into the bag, expertly guided by Emily Hope.

Nicole held the bag tightly with both hands. 'Phew!' she said. 'Sorry about that! Thanks so much for your help. I'd better get him home right away.'

'He'll be fine,' Emily Hope said reassuringly as Nicole headed for the door. 'Just don't let him get away in the High Street!'

When Nicole had gone, Mrs Hope gave a big sigh. 'What a day!' she said, firmly latching the surgery front door. 'I need a cup of tea.' She turned to Mandy. 'Was that Craig I glimpsed dashing through here?'

'Yes,' Mandy said. 'But then he headed straight out again.'

'Well, I'm sure he'll come back when he's hungry,' said Emily Hope. 'I'm going to have lunch, and then there are piles of paperwork to sort out. Coming?'

The first chance Mandy had for talking with her parents about Ming was over supper that evening. They were gathered around the kitchen table, tucking into a delicious stirfry. Craig had not appeared and, when Mr Hope suggested that

Mandy might like to knock on his door, she declined.

'No, Dad,' she said pleadingly, not relishing the task. 'I really think he just wants to be left alone. He hasn't spent a minute with us since we got here.'

'He must be hungry,' Mr Hope pointed out. 'I think he ought to eat something.'

'I'll take him up something on a tray a bit later,' said Emily Hope, passing James another helping of salad. 'Let's leave him in peace.'

Mandy didn't want to think about Craig. She was curious and a little bit worried about his odd behaviour, but she was determined that he was not going to spoil their excitement over entering Ming in the show.

'Mr Allardyce has said that James and I can enter Ming in the show!' she reported happily, changing the subject.

'The gorgeous Siamese that came into surgery yesterday?' said Mrs Hope. 'Well, I would think she has as good a chance as any.'

'Do you?' James asked eagerly. 'Do you really? Only, you see, Appleheads are not so popular these days. Judges favour the more modern-looking Wedgehead Siamese who are—'

'Slow down!' Mrs Hope held up a hand, laughing. 'James, you sound as if you have been studying the breed books I brought with me!'

'But it's true,' Mandy said sadly. 'Mrs Stewart and Mr Allardyce told us that modern Siamese are all the rage now, and the traditional shape and colour of the Appleheads are appearing less and less often in shows.'

'So we really want to enter Ming,' James went on. 'It's not fair that the Wedgehead Siamese are getting all the attention.'

'I absolutely agree,' said Emily Hope. 'Let Ming stand up for her breed at the show.'

'Great!' Mandy cried. 'What do we have to do before the show?'

'Do?' said Adam Hope. 'Not much – except let Mum check that her eyes are clear and bright again. That's all there is to it.'

'Brush her, obviously,' Mrs Hope mused. 'And generally make sure she's in the best possible condition. I'll give the show secretary a ring in the morning. We'll have to fill out an entry form for Ming.'

'Oh, I can't wait!' Mandy stood up. 'Can James and I have a look at your cat manuals? I want to know everything there is to know.'

'Of course,' Mrs Hope replied. '*After* you've washed the dishes,' she added, her eyes sparkling.

Mandy found the pile of manuals on show cats in her parents' room. She and James sat cross-legged on the carpet at the foot of the bed and began leafing through one on cat showing.

'Exemption, sanction and championship,' he read, his glasses slipping down his nose in the warm summer night air. 'Sounds confusing.'

'We need to read up about championship,' Mandy said knowledgeably. 'That's the one we're interested in. You see, it says here that—'

The shrill ringing of the phone on the bedside table interrupted her. Mandy got up to answer it. 'Hello?'

'Is that Mandy, by any chance?' asked a faint voice.

'Yes,' she said. 'This is Mandy Hope.'

'Hello, Mandy, this is Anna MacLeod. I'm phoning from Italy. Is your mother there, or your dad?'

'Um, I'm afraid my mum's in the bath,' Mandy said. 'And Dad has gone out on a call.'

'Oh, well, it doesn't matter, really. I just wondered how Craig was getting on?'

Mandy froze, her thoughts racing. Should she let Craig's mother know about his strange behaviour? She didn't want to tell tales, but he did seem to be unhappy and Mandy was worried about him.

'I don't think he's doing well at all,' she blurted out. On the floor, James turned sharply to look at her and his eyebrows shot up.

'What?' said Mrs MacLeod. 'Why? He's not ill, is he?'

'No.' Mandy hesitated, unsure of what she should say. James had covered his face with both hands and was shaking his head as if to warn her to say nothing.

'Maybe I shouldn't say anything, Mrs MacLeod,' Mandy went on, 'but he really seems unhappy. I'd like to be his friend, but he doesn't seem to want to have anything to do with me . . . us,' she finished, turning away from James, who had pretended to faint in dismay. He was lying flat out on the carpet.

'Oh, poor Mandy,' Anna MacLeod said sympathetically. Her voice sounded small, and very far away. 'You must be confused! I'm sorry Craig is being antisocial. It has taken him a while to adjust to having to leave Scotland, his friends and his school. He never wanted to move to Jersey, you see.'

'Oh,' said Mandy. 'I didn't know that. We were in surgery today, with Nicole Stewart's pet snake Kellogg, and Craig came in and then he charged through the waiting room and up the stairs as though . . .'

'Snake?' Mrs MacLeod repeated, speaking over Mandy. 'Did you say snake?'

'Yes, Kellogg. He's a corn snake.'

'Oh, dear. Craig is petrified of snakes!' his mother exclaimed. 'When he was little, he went away to a summer camp and was bitten by an adder. He had to be rushed to hospital and he never got over the shock.'

'Gosh, how awful!' Mandy said. 'Was he hurt?'

'I think it stung, but he responded quickly to treatment,' Anna MacLeod explained. 'He was just very frightened; he was only five at the time,' she went on. 'I sometimes think it was then that he decided not to have anything further to do with animals. He tries to avoid them as much as he can, which isn't easy with vets for parents.'

Mandy felt a pang of sympathy for Craig. She

couldn't imagine living in a veterinary surgery and not liking animals! That must be why he didn't help out with any of the chores.

James began waving his arms about to distract her. When she turned, she saw her father standing in the doorway, his eyebrows raised enquiringly.

'Who is it?' he whispered.

'Oh, Mrs MacLeod?' Mandy said. 'My dad's here now. I'll pass you over. Bye.'

'Bye, Mandy – and thanks for being concerned about Craig. I'm sure he'll be fine, but seeing that snake today would have given him a shock, that's for sure!'

Mandy gave Mr Hope the telephone, then beckoned to James to follow her out of the room.

'Why did you have to tell her about Craig being so moody?' James groaned. 'You shouldn't have said anything. He'll be so cross with us!'

'No, it was really helpful. Mrs MacLeod said that he was scared of snakes,' Mandy said. 'Apparently, he's found it hard to settle here after being in Scotland, so I guess the last thing he wanted was for his mum and dad to go away without him – and seeing Kellogg must have been the last straw!' She led the way to the kitchen.

The room was dark and Mandy had to grope along the wall looking for the switch. As soon as the lights were on, James made a beeline for a big tin on the table.

'I feel really sorry for him,' Mandy went on.

'Me too,' James agreed, his hand in the biscuit tin. 'But what more can we do to show him we want to be friends?'

Mandy was about to answer when a noise behind her made her turn around. Craig had appeared at the door. He frowned when he saw them. 'Oh, hi,' he said.

'Hi,' Mandy and James said together.

Craig was in his dressing gown, his dark hair wet from the shower. He walked over to the fridge and opened it, looking for something.

'Do you want to come for a walk with Noodles tomorrow?' James asked him. 'We might go to the beach.'

Craig straightened up, a pint of milk in his hand. 'No, thanks,' he replied, without turning round.

Mandy suddenly felt hot with a mix of concern and annoyance. They were only trying to be friendly!

'Are you still worried about seeing the snake?' she asked.

Craig spun round and stared at her, horrified. 'What do you mean? Why should I be worried?'

'Well . . . I . . .' Mandy stammered. She couldn't tell Craig that she had spoken to his mother about him.

James sat down at the table and examined his biscuit closely.

'Look, it's none of your business, all right?' snapped Craig, pouring the milk into a glass so quickly it spilled.

'But it *is*,' Mandy persisted bravely. 'It *is* my business – because we'd like to be friends!'

Craig put the glass of milk on the counter. 'Well, you can start by leaving me alone,' he growled. 'Just because you love animals doesn't mean everyone has to. Not everyone is like you! So stop interfering, OK? Just stop interfering!' And with that he stormed to the door and stamped up the stairs.

'Oh, no,' groaned James. 'Now look what you've done.'

Mandy sat down beside him and propped her chin in her hands. 'Yes,' she said sadly. 'I've really ruined things now, haven't I?'

Eight

On Monday morning, Mandy got up a soon as she heard her mother moving around. There was the comforting chink of the teapot lid and the familiar sound of Emily Hope's slippers scuffing softly on the floor. Mandy joined her.

'Hello, love,' Mrs Hope greeted her. 'You're up early.'

'I didn't sleep very well,' Mandy said, giving her mother a hug. 'I think I might have upset Craig.'

'Upset him? How?' Emily Hope looked puzzled. She picked up Craig's abandoned glass, sniffed the soured milk, then poured it down the sink.

Mandy folded her arms and rested her back against the larder door. She related the story Anna MacLeod had shared with her about Craig's ordeal with the snake, and confessed how she had suddenly taken it into her head to confront Craig about his fears.

'I only want to be friends,' Mandy ended miserably. 'Now he's really mad.'

Emily Hope put an arm around Mandy's shoulders and pushed her tousled fair hair off her forehead. 'I don't think so. I think he knows you'd like to include him. I should behave as though nothing has happened. You've given him something to think about and no harm has been done.'

'Thanks, Mum.' Mandy felt better as she realised there was nothing else she could do. She just hoped Craig didn't mind too much that she knew about his snake phobia.

'What are you and James going to do today?' Emily Hope asked, changing the subject.

'We're going to go and see Mrs Stewart and ask her to give us some tips on how to make Ming even more perfect for the show.' Mandy smiled; thinking of Ming gave her a warm, happy feeling. She put Craig to the back of her mind and decided to go and wake James. There was Noodles to walk, too. It was going to be a busy day.

Mrs Stewart was out in her garden, pruning a shrub into a smoothly rounded ball. She seemed pleased at the chance for a break from the hot morning sun.

'How's Kellogg?' Mandy asked.

'He's perked up no end,' she answered, pulling off her gardening gloves and tossing them on to a patio chair. 'Nicole, on the other hand, is working far too hard and *still* hasn't come up with a suitable idea for her theme for Saturday. She's very frustrated.'

'She must be,' Mandy sympathised, noticing Gateau's portly frame gliding through the undergrowth. 'There's Gateau, James. Look at his twitching tail!'

'I'm sure he thinks he's about to pounce on some unsuspecting prey,' Mrs Stewart laughed. 'But it's very unlikely, at his age.'

'We've come to ask you for some tips on grooming Ming for the show,' James told her.

Mrs Stewart smiled broadly. 'Thomas has agreed? How wonderful!'

'Well,' Mandy corrected her, 'he agreed to let *us* enter and show Ming. So, you see, it's all down to James and me.'

'Well, I'll let you have Gateau's equipment. They're distantly related, so I'm sure he won't mind! You can take it over to Thomas's and begin getting Ming in shape right away,' Mrs Stewart said, her eyes shining. 'How wonderful! Come with me.'

James and Mandy followed Mrs Stewart into the house. On a shelf in the study was a sealed plastic box marked 'Gateau'. She prized open the lid and began lifting out a series of shiny gold medallions, curled glossy ribbons and a collection of implements Mandy could not name.

'Grooming a cat takes lots of patience,' Mrs Stewart advised. 'Some don't like it much, others love it. It just depends on the cat.'

Mandy spotted a framed photograph of Gateau on the wall. There was no mistaking the proud expression on his face. His smoothly muscular body was glowing with good health, his chin was high and, in profile, he seemed to be smiling.

'This is a bristle brush,' Mrs Stewart told them, holding out something that looked like a small body brush used on horses. 'It's used on short-haired cats to remove any loose, dead fur. And this is a wide-toothed comb to take out any matted hair from the coat – though if Ming has any, especially under her tummy, you may be able to tease it out gently with your fingers. Don't forget to trim her nails if they're long. The judges will look for good nails. This is the little clipper you'll need, but I expect your parents will help you with that, Mandy. Also, a pair of nail scissors for tiny clumps in the coat. Brush in the direction the hair grows and don't forget the belly and legs, will you?' she prompted.

'We won't,' James said solemnly. 'Thanks.' He took the bag into which Mrs Stewart had packed the grooming items.

'Yes, thank you,' Mandy echoed, newly fired up by the pictures of Gateau and the thought of using the grooming kit on Ming. 'We're going to do our best to remind people just how fantastic Appleheads are!'

As Mandy and James went through the doorway to Mr Allardyce's shop, they heard him muttering. 'Shoo, shoo, Noodles. Stop bothering Ming like this. Go and find your own sunny spot, there's a good boy.'

'Hello, Mr Allardyce,' Mandy called.

The elderly man looked up from the window display area and waved. 'Here's the cavalry to the rescue – just in time!' He smiled. 'Noodles is being particularly bothersome today. He won't give Ming a minute's peace.'

Mandy peered over a chest of drawers at Ming. She seemed determined to keep her spot in the window, still warm from the morning sun, but she was looking warily at Noodles, her blue eyes bright.

'Would she mind us practising grooming her?' Mandy asked. 'Mrs Stewart has lent us Gateau's brushes and combs.'

'I'll distract Noodles,' James offered. 'I can play with him while you tackle Ming.'

Mandy looked gratefully at him. 'Great, James. I'll have a go at this, and then we can take Noodles for a walk on the beach.'

'Pick her up, Mandy,' Mr Allardyce suggested. 'She'd like a bit of fuss. You can bring her through to the back room. I've got a table in there that should be just the right height for grooming her.'

Mandy gently scooped Ming into her arms. The cat was as limp and soft as a toy, snuggling against

Mandy's chest. As her triangular pink nose touched her chin, Mandy could feel Ming's soft breath on her cheek as she carried her.

'Here we are,' said Thomas Allardyce, picking up a stack of magazines from the table. Mandy kissed Ming's silky head and lowered her on to the plastic tablecloth. She meowed and looked around in great interest. As each instrument was brought out of Mrs Stewart's bag, Ming smelled it carefully and made a series of little noises ranging from a rumble to a delighted purr.

'I have a customer,' Mr Allardyce told Mandy as the doorbell rang in the shop, 'so I'll leave you to it, shall I?'

'That's fine, Mr Allardyce,' Mandy answered.

'Sit, Noodles!' she heard James command behind her. 'Now, give me your paw!'

Mandy chuckled as she drew the grooming brush over Ming's fur. She could feel the ridge of the cat's delicate spine under the bristles and was careful not to press too hard.

'Does she like it?' James called and Mandy half-turned to see him lying on the floor, Noodles prancing around him like a great shaggy bear. 'Er, I've given up with the dog training,' he added

sheepishly, pushing Noodles away as he tried to
lick James's spectacles.

'She seems to,' Mandy said, 'judging by the
purring!'

Ming stretched and turned, then rolled over
and put her front paws on to the comb. With a
skilful flick she sent it spinning on to the floor.
When Mandy reached down to get it back, Ming
sat up on the table and looked at her, a spark of
mischief in her blue eyes. As Mandy began to

straighten up, Ming reached out and patted Mandy on the top of her head.

'You're a sweetie,' Mandy told her, kissing the cat on the nose so that Ming gave a delicate sneeze. 'You never put your claws out, do you?'

'What?' said James, adding, 'Oh, Noodles! Don't do that!'

'Nothing,' Mandy laughed. 'Ming's being very good, that's all.'

The Siamese cat lay on her side while Mandy ran the comb along her flank. Her coat was shining now, soft as silk, and Mandy felt pleased with her efforts. She looked around her, thinking that she could have stayed there with Ming for ever. Above the table, up on the wall, was one of Thomas Allardyce's framed photographs of a basketful of kittens. There were eight of them, Mandy counted, peeping out over the rim, and the photographer had perfectly captured the curiosity and naughtiness of kittens' expressions. Hanging beside it was a watercolour painting of a ginger tabby cat on a wicker chair.

'Beaumont is filled with cat lovers,' Mandy thought, as she picked the tiniest brush of all to do Ming's ears. Suddenly, she had an idea that made her heart leap with the brilliance of it. Mr Allardyce's collection of cat pictures would provide the perfect backdrop for the walls of Nicole's hotel! They would be an ideal talking point for the guests as they arrived. Mandy was so excited that she almost called out to him, but he was busy at the other end of the shop with a customer and she thought better of it. Mr Allardyce had already agreed to let them enter Ming in the show. Perhaps it would be better to talk to Nicole first and see what she thought.

'Mandy, Noodles is getting restless,' James announced, coming up behind her. He was out of breath and his glasses were at an angle. 'I think I'd better take him out.'

'I'm just finished with Ming,' Mandy said. 'She's gone all drowsy from the brushing. I'll put her back in the window and come with you.'

Noodles seemed thrilled to be going for a walk. He stepped along proudly, not tugging quite so hard at his lead. He was putting more pressure on the injured foot and had almost succeeded in shredding the grubby bandage with his teeth. As they passed the door to Mrs Gibb's shop, James waved.

Mrs Gibb waved back, smiling, and called out, 'Thanks so much!'

Mandy told James about her idea for Nicole's hotel display. 'There must be eighty pictures, if not more,' she said. 'Wouldn't it be brilliant?'

'It would,' James acknowledged, 'but d'you think Mr Allardyce would agree? They're his pride and joy, those pictures.'

'Well, no harm would come to them,' Mandy reasoned. 'I don't see why not.'

'Look!' James pointed and stopped short. 'There's Nicole now. Why don't we ask her?'

Nicole was hurrying towards them, looking harassed. She was carrying a large cardboard box.

'Nicole!' Mandy caught her attention.

'Hi,' she said. 'Whew! Isn't it hot?'

'We're taking Noodles to the beach,' said James.

'Have a dip for me,' said Nicole, sounding envious. 'I've got to get back to the hotel.' She lifted the box. 'These are new wine glasses. We ran out.'

'Wait,' Mandy pleaded, as Nicole stepped around them. 'We've got an idea for your welcome theme. We think it might be really good.'

Nicole shifted the box to her hip. 'OK, what's your idea?'

'Have you seen Mr Allardyce's cats?' James began.

Nicole looked surprised. 'You mean Ming?'

'No, no!' Mandy smiled. 'His cat art – his pictures. He's got tonnes of brilliant pictures, drawings and paintings of cats everywhere!'

'In the shop?' Nicole cocked her head, seeming more and more interested.

'Yes, all over the walls. If you asked him, I'll bet he'd lend them to you,' Mandy finished, crossing her arms in triumph.

'How many are there?' Nicole took off her sunglasses with her free hand. 'Enough to cover a hotel lobby and dining room?'

'I'm sure,' Mandy said.

'That's fantastic!' Nicole grinned. 'I'll talk to my manager. Now I'd better hurry back to work.'

Nicole set out at a brisk pace, her high-heeled sandals tip-tapping on the pavement. 'You might have saved the day!' she called back over her shoulder.

Mandy's spirits were high as she and James crossed the road and ran down the steps to the beach. She felt positive that Ming would make a great impression at the show, and now it looked as though they had helped Nicole, too.

They took off their shoes and James let Noodle off the lead. He barked joyfully, turning in circles to show his appreciation, then blundering into an abandoned sandcastle. They started running across the burning sand towards the water, dodging the brightly coloured beach umbrellas. The dog bounded into the water, allowing the waves to swirl around him, cooling his tummy.

'Oh, that's nice,' said James, when the water splashed up around his knees. 'Let's spend the rest of the day right here.'

Mandy nodded and fished in the pocket of her shorts to bring out a couple of coins. 'I've even got enough money for ice creams,' she declared happily.

Noodles was exhausted by the time they came back up from the beach. His pink tongue lolled as he walked sedately at James's side. As soon as they reached Mrs Gibb's back door, he went straight into his basket and collapsed with a big sigh.

'This is for you,' said Mrs Gibb, holding out a large, sticky chocolate cake. 'I made it to say thank you to you both.'

'Oh! What a fantastic cake!' Mandy said.

'Yum!' James's eyes lit up. 'Thanks!'

Mandy and James gave Noodles a farewell pat and carried the cake back to the surgery. As they opened the door to the house, Mandy felt a pang of worry. Would Craig still be angry with her, she wondered?

'What have you got there!' exclaimed Adam Hope, as they came in.

Mandy set the cake down. 'A present from Mrs Gibb for walking Noodles,' she said.

'How nice!' Emily Hope smiled. 'Would anyone like a piece for tea?'

'Yes, please!' James said quickly.

'I've got good news,' said Adam Hope. 'Mrs Sullivan rang a little while ago to say that Katie the calf is much better, and eating normally.'

'Oh, good!' Mandy said.

'Now, tell us all about your day,' Adam Hope prompted, as he found a suitable knife to cut the cake.

'Yes,' Mandy's mother agreed. 'But first, Mandy, would you take some cake up to Craig? I'm sure he'd like a piece. He's in his room.'

Mandy's heart sank. She felt really nervous after their quarrel the night before, but she knew she had to make an effort. 'OK,' she said, and caught James's eye. He raised his eyebrows at her.

Mandy carried the small plate up the stairs to the top of the house. There was music coming from inside Craig's room, so she knocked quite hard on the door. It opened and Craig looked out at her, his face expressionless.

'For you,' Mandy said, trying to muster a smile.

Craig's eyes fell on the deliciously gooey, dark chocolate cake. 'I'm not hungry, thank you,' he said, and firmly shut the door.

Mandy's shoulders slumped. She turned and trudged down the stairs. 'I give up,' she said to herself. 'I just give up!'

There was little sign of Craig over the next two days. Mandy couldn't help feeling relieved, but she was still worried about him. He was such a loner! Her mum tried to reassure her when Mandy said how concerned she was.

'He's fine,' Emily Hope said. 'He seems really busy with his soccer practice. I'm sure he's OK, love. He just prefers his own company.'

Mandy and James had soon found that they were as busy with the routine on Jersey as they had been back home in Welford. They helped in the surgery and the residential unit, walked Noodles and played with Ming – and spent time on the beach. Eventually, Mandy had to admit that it was hard to worry too much about Craig when they were having such a lovely time.

Nicole had been to see Thomas Allardyce and he had readily agreed to allow his collection to hang in the hotel foyer on the day of the show. When Nicole rang Mandy to thank her, she sounded thrilled.

'It's a great idea, really super, Mandy,' she enthused. 'They're going to look just right.'

'I'm so pleased,' Mandy said happily. 'We'll definitely come and see them when they're hanging in the hotel.'

'Have you and James had a cream tea yet?' Nicole asked suddenly.

'Yes, but we wouldn't mind another!' Mandy said. 'Why?'

'I want to say thank you,' Nicole explained. 'Come and have a cream tea at my house tomorrow, say, four o'clock?'

'Thanks!' Mandy said, winking at James, who was hovering near the phone, trying to listen in.

'I'll invite Mr Allardyce, and why don't you bring your parents – and Craig?' Nicole added. 'We can have a pre-cat-show party!'

'Um . . . OK, thank you,' Mandy said. 'We'll see you tomorrow.' She replaced the receiver.

'Not Mrs MacLeod?' James groaned.

'No, Nicole Stewart.' Mandy grinned. 'We're going to a pre-cat-show cream tea.'

'Hooray!' said James.

On Thursday morning, during breakfast, Mandy's mother managed to persuade Craig that he should go with them to the Stewarts for tea. He seemed reluctant and, when it was time to leave, he walked a pace or two behind the others as they made their way to the house.

'Thank heavens for Jennifer,' said Adam Hope, fanning his face with a straw hat. 'It's too hot to be in surgery today.'

'Yes,' Mrs Hope agreed. 'But we have no bookings, so it should be peaceful enough. She'll ring us if there's an emergency.'

Mrs Stewart and Nicole had set up a table under the awning of the patio. Thomas Allardyce was busy gathering chairs and placing them in a circle.

A small breeze stirred the edges of a pretty cloth and James's eyes bulged when he saw a towering pile of scones, still steaming from the oven.

'Wow!' said Mandy. 'This looks amazing.'

'There's clotted-cream ice cream a bit later, if you've got room,' Mrs Stewart said as they took their seats.

Gateau was lying in the shade of a chair, stretched out to his fullest on the cool flagstone patio.

'Ming is indoors,' said Thomas Allardyce. 'She's not a great one for the heat.'

'Do cats suffer in the heat?' James asked. 'I mean, they don't sweat, do they?'

'You're right, James,' said Mrs Stewart. 'Dogs perspire by panting but cats can't perspire at all. So they keep cool by doing very little on hot days. They lie around in the coolest places they can find.'

'That reminds me,' Mr Allardyce said, passing around the plate of scones. 'I delivered the last box of cat pictures to your hotel this morning, Nicole.'

'Oh, thank you!' said Nicole. 'It's going to look brilliant when they're all hung up on the walls – just like an art gallery dedicated to cats!'

'I like the picture of the Victorian lady wheeling

her cat in a pram,' said James, taking the bowl of strawberry jam Mrs Stewart offered him.

'Me too,' said Mandy. Then she frowned. She had heard a faint but distinctive cry. 'What's that?' It might have been a child, or a gull . . .

'What's what?' asked James.

'Shh!' Mandy urged him, holding up her hand. Everyone stared at her. There it was again, a long, high whine that ended on a desperate note. Mandy strained to make sense of it, but her heart had begun a dull, fearful thudding. She heard the cry for a third time, this time sounding more urgent still. It was a sound she recognised with sudden, heart-stopping clarity.

'That's Ming!' she cried. 'I know it is. Something's wrong!'

Mandy's chair thudded to the ground as she rushed away from the table. She was down the steps of the patio and across the garden in a second and racing to wrench open the gate that led to the lane that ran behind the row of houses. She narrowly avoided a boy on a bicycle, who wobbled dangerously as she burst out and ran towards Mr Allardyce's shop.

To her horror, she saw thin, dark grey plumes of

smoke coiling from the cracks of the back door of
Allardyce Antiques.

'Fire!' Mandy shouted, as loudly as she could.
'Help! Fire!'

Nine

The smoke seeping around the door thickened as Mandy watched helplessly. She grabbed the handle of the locked door and rattled it, listening in dismay to the repeated yowling of the Siamese inside.

'*Ming*!' Mandy peered through the kitchen window of the burning shop. 'Oh, please be safe, Ming.' With her nose pressed against the glass and her trembling hands cupped around her face, she could see bright orange flames and billowing smoke. There was no sign of Ming.

Mandy frantically looked left and right, wondering if she should try and break the window.

But then she heard footsteps on the path behind her and turned to see Thomas Allardyce with a big bunch of keys.

'The fire brigade is on its way,' shouted James, pelting past in the lane. 'I'll go and warn Mrs Gibb.'

Mandy saw her parents running towards the surgery. 'We're going to evacuate the residential unit in case it spreads,' Adam Hope called.

'I'll give you a hand,' Mrs Stewart shouted, and began to run to catch up. 'Nicole's gone to the house on the other side.'

Mr Allardyce looked down at Mandy. 'It looks like it's just you and me here, then,' he said. He unlocked the door and pushed it open, putting out an arm to keep Mandy back. Mandy was far too sensible to risk running into the shop; what she wanted was an escape route for Ming!

From among the clutter on the floor, amid the swirl of smoke and the crackle of the flames, a small dark face appeared, wide eyed with terror. Ming gave a piteous wail and slunk towards safety. As she dashed out of the door, Mandy bent down and gathered her up into her arms.

'Ming! Oh, Ming, you're all right!' she said, burying her face in the cat's smoke-stained coat.

Ming's body was tense with fright, but, as Mandy soothed her, she began to relax. She sneezed once, then again, and pushed herself higher until her nose was touching Mandy's ear. Mandy's hair covered the cat's face like a curtain. The cat's breathing was rapid and warm and it tickled Mandy's neck. Ming snuggled there, finding comfort in a place where she could no longer smell the acrid smoke. Mandy marvelled that, frightened though she was, Ming hadn't once used her claws to cling on.

When Thomas Allardyce had made certain that his beloved cat was safe, he made a grab for the fire extinguisher hanging above the hob and went into his shop. Mandy gave a sigh of relief as she heard the first faint wail of a fire engine heading their way. She decided to take Ming to Mrs Stewart's house. It was very close and seeing Gateau might help Ming to calm down.

'Come on,' she said softly. 'I'm going to get you away from all this noise and confusion, poor girl.'

Mandy wondered if the cat would panic when she began walking down the road. She could hear the fire engine pulling up on the main street with its alarm wailing. But Ming stayed exactly where she was, hiding under Mandy's hair, her front paws warm around her neck. When they reached Mrs Stewart's back door, the cat peeped out to see where she was and gave a third, delicate sneeze.

'You've inhaled a bit of smoke,' Mandy told her, reaching out to open the door. But someone was already there. The door flew open, so hard that Mandy had to jump back to avoid colliding with it. Craig bolted out of the door just as Mrs Stewart and Mandy's mother came in through the gate from the lane.

'Goodness!' said Mrs Stewart, stopping short with surprise. 'Are you all right, Craig?'

There was a sudden silence. Craig stood there, shifting unhappily from foot to foot. His arms were straight out in front of him, rigid, a heavy black and orange loop coiled around his wrist. Mandy felt her mouth drop open in astonishment when she realised what he was carrying. Craig was holding the corn snake! Kellogg's head swayed from side to side in alarmed confusion, his split tongue going nineteen to the dozen. Even to Mandy, the corn snake's posture appeared a little menacing. How must he appear to a boy who was petrified of snakes?

'Take him!' Craig begged, as Nicole suddenly arrived in the garden. She was heaving for breath, her eyes wide with concern, and Mandy saw that the heel of one of her shoes was broken.

'Kellogg!' Nicole breathed, and took the snake as Craig thrust him at her. He had to shake his wrist free of the tail end.

'Quick! I'm going back in for the cat. I saw him in the kitchen!' he said at once.

'Gateau?' said Mrs Stewart, puzzled.

Mrs Hope put her hand on Craig's arm. 'It's all right, Craig,' she said quietly. 'The fire is under control – it won't spread to Mrs Stewart's house. You can leave Gateau where he is.'

Craig flushed. 'Oh, right,' he said.

Mandy was so surprised by what Craig had done that she didn't know what to say. What incredible courage he had shown, dashing in to rescue the animals from the fire he had thought was about to spread into their home! Mandy could hardly believe it. She wanted to give him a hug to thank him, but she was too shy. Besides, Craig was still looking quite cross.

'Look out!' Everyone turned as the shout echoed down the lane. Mandy recognised James's voice and, in spite of everything, she began to smile.

'Stop!' James yelled weakly, coming into view in the lane. 'Do as you're told!'

Noodles came bouncing through the gate, his tongue lolling and his ears flapping up and down. James was seconds behind, looking defeated and very hot.

'He slipped his lead,' he explained sheepishly. 'Mrs Gibb wasn't there, so I took him, only he got loose.'

Mrs Hope was trying not to laugh. She put her arm around James's shoulders. Noodles greeted everyone in turn, then hurried over to inspect the only person he didn't really know well – Craig. The dog put his nose into Craig's palm and sniffed it with great interest. Mandy held her breath, wondering what Craig would do. As she watched, he put a hesitant hand on Noodles' head. Noodles sat down, pressing up close against Craig's legs, and looked up at him with warm, loving eyes.

Mandy's eyes filled with sudden tears. She blinked them away. 'You're a hero,' she said simply, smiling at Craig. 'Even Noodles knows that.'

'Not me,' he replied, his fingers playing with

Noodles' curly coat. '*You*, maybe. I saw you trying to get into the burning shop. You'd do anything daft to save the life of an animal.'

For an instant, Mandy wondered if Craig was making fun of her, but, when she looked at him, she saw that he was looking directly back at her and that his eyes were twinkling in a kind way.

'Yes, well done, Craig!' said Mrs Stewart.

'Thanks for rescuing Kellogg!' Nicole put in.

'*You* rescued the snake?' asked James, looking from Craig to Mandy. When Mandy nodded. James's eyebrows shot up.

'Well, not really. When Mandy took off, all of you rushed next door,' Craig explained, shrugging. 'I thought the fire might come this way and that I'd better get the pets out. I found the snake in that glass case but it looked too heavy to carry, so I just took him out. I hope that's OK?' he added nervously.

'Absolutely! A courageous decision,' said Mrs Stewart. 'Now, let's all go inside and settle the animals. Then we'll go back and see if Thomas needs our help.'

'Good idea,' Mandy said. Ming still lay sleepily against her shoulder, her blue eyes half-closed.

Mandy loved her fiercely. She felt very proud that Ming had been the one to raise the alarm in the first place.

'I think that Siamese cat deserves a special thank you,' said Craig as he went into the house behind her.

'Ming,' Mandy said, turning and smiling. 'Her name is Ming.'

'Ming,' Craig corrected himself. 'She's a clever cat, that's for sure.'

'I agree,' Mandy grinned. 'A very clever – and beautiful – cat!'

They hadn't long been crowded into Mrs Stewart's sitting room when Adam Hope and Thomas Allardyce appeared.

'Thomas!' Mrs Stewart gasped, hugging her friend. 'We're so sorry for you. Is there much damage?'

Mr Allardyce looked very weary. The pocket of his shirt had been ripped and he had a black smudge across his forehead. He shook his head. 'Not much, Deborah,' he replied, gratefully accepting a chair. 'The fire brigade are dealing with it now – the flames are well under control.'

'What happened?' Nicole asked.

'It seems the sun is to blame,' said Adam Hope, rubbing his cheek and leaving a sooty black mark. 'The fire was started by sunshine hitting the lens of a magnifying glass lying in the window! It's a good thing Thomas wasn't very far away or the whole shop might have gone up.'

'Thank you, Mandy,' said Mr Allardyce. 'If you hadn't heard Ming call out . . .' His voice shook and he trailed off.

'We should thank Ming,' Mandy said, putting out her hand to the Siamese who was curled up on a cushion on the sofa. Ming gave a little rumble in acknowledgment.

'You know, that window sill has been a little unlucky all round,' Mr Allardyce said, recovering himself. 'Nothing but trouble!' He glared playfully at Noodles, who was sitting beside Craig. The dog looked up and fixed Mr Allardyce with a beady eye, then wagged his stumpy tail.

'You'll have to make a temporary place for Ming in the shop while the window sill is rebuilt,' Mandy suggested. 'Somewhere Noodles can't reach!'

'Good idea,' Mr Allardyce agreed. 'Though it will have to be a spot in the sun.'

'I'm very glad that there's no serious damage to anything or anyone,' said Nicole, reaching out to stroke Gateau as he stalked past. Mandy thought that the elderly cat looked a bit put out by all the upheaval around him.

'And it's a good thing that Mr Allardyce's collection of cat pictures were not still hanging inside the shop,' Mandy remarked.

'Goodness, yes,' said Mrs Stewart. 'The smoke would have ruined them.'

There was a knock on the front door and Nicole got up to open it. Sarah Jane Gibb stood there, looking flustered.

'Is everybody all right?' she asked anxiously. 'Noodles . . . ?'

'Everybody's fine,' Nicole assured her, stepping aside to let her in. 'James went to fetch Noodles the moment the fire started.'

'Oh, thank you!' Mrs Gibb looked around at the gathering in the sitting room. Noodles hurried over to jump up and lick her face. 'It seems I'm never around when I'm needed! I'd gone out to do a bit of shopping. I'm so sorry about the shop, Thomas.'

'No real harm done, Sarah Jane,' said Mr Allardyce.

'Sit down,' Mrs Stewart urged her. 'I'll get the rest of that cream tea we began, and we'll tell you all about it!'

Ten

When Mandy woke up on Saturday morning it was clear and bright, and much cooler than before. She noticed the change in temperature right away and felt glad. She wanted Ming to be as comfortable as possible on her big day. In spite of the fire, the Siamese was looking in peak condition and Mandy's mum had pronounced her completely fit. Excitement fluttered through Mandy as she dressed. It would be brilliant if Ming won a prize!

In the kitchen, her dad and James were tucking into a stack of pancakes. To Mandy's surprise,

Craig was sitting at the table too, dribbling honey from a spoon on to his pancake.

'Hi,' Mandy said casually, acting as though Craig had joined them for breakfast every day. He gave her a quick smile as she sat down. Mrs Hope delivered a pancake to her plate with a small plop.

'Dad and I have a patient to see in surgery,' she said. 'We won't be long. We plan to leave for the show around lunchtime, OK?'

Mandy nodded. 'James and I will collect Ming and have her ready by then.'

'Mrs Stewart is going to help us,' James added.

'Good. We'll see you later.' Mr Hope plunged the frying pan into a basin of cold water with a sizzle and followed Mandy's mum out of the room.

When they'd gone, Mandy felt a little shyness creep over her again. But, to her surprise, Craig seemed far more relaxed.

'My dad rang this morning,' he said. 'I told him about the fire – and Kellogg.'

'What did he say?' Mandy asked.

Craig glanced down at his half-eaten pancake. 'He couldn't believe I'd handled that snake! I guess he was pleased, though.'

'I bet he was,' James commented.

'I'm sorry I've been such a pain,' Craig said suddenly, looking up again. 'Ever since I ended up in hospital after that snakebite I've tried my best to keep away from animals. But somehow, on Thursday, it was different.'

'How?' asked James, frowning.

'I don't know, really.' Craig ran his fingers through his curly hair. 'I was so focused on trying to save lives during that fire I didn't stop to think that I might be putting myself in danger. I just did it.'

'It must be hard,' Mandy said sympathetically. 'I mean, I've grown up with animals and I love them, but I know not everyone feels the same way.'

Craig shot her a grateful look from under his dark fringe. 'You're right,' he agreed. 'Leaving Scotland and saying goodbye to my friends, my school and my football team was really difficult. I guess I was pretty resentful.'

'Do you think you'll feel differently from now on?' James prompted.

'Differently?' Craig thought for a moment. 'Well, not different, but maybe it'll be easier to be around the animals that come into the surgery. I mean, I've kind of proved to myself that I can handle snakes – and dogs – so I guess I can cope with anything!'

'Animals can sense fear in people,' Mandy pointed out. 'They seem to know when people are not comfortable with them and don't trust them.'

Craig laughed. 'Well, I *didn't* trust Kellogg not to bite me when I grabbed him out of that tank!'

'That makes you even more brave,' Mandy said.

'Yes, really,' James said admiringly. He added, 'Corn snakes don't bite, you know.'

Mandy finished her pancake. 'James and I must go and get Ming ready for the show. Are you coming?'

'No,' Craig said, taking his plate to the sink. 'I've got a football game.' He turned and grinned at them. 'But I'll be there to congratulate Ming when you get back.'

'Cross fingers,' Mandy said, grinning.

'Good luck,' Craig called as they went into the hall.

James nudged Mandy and gave her a thumbs-up sign. She smiled broadly at him. It looked like Craig was going to be OK after all.

* * *

'Right here,' said Mrs Stewart, turning Ming so that Mandy could clip away an uneven bit of her coat. 'And look, there's a tiny matt of fur between those toes.'

Mandy was concentrating hard, wielding the small scissors very carefully so as not to stab Ming with their sharp points. The Siamese was lying on her side on the table in Mr Allardyce's back room, purring loudly. Every so often she raised her leg and began doing her own grooming. Mandy could hear the rasping of the cat's rough tongue on her coat.

'Now for her ears,' Mr Allardyce urged, leaning over to have a look at his cat. 'They should be pink and clean.' There were no customers in the shop, so he had come to watch the preparations for the show.

'Are her eyes clear?' James asked. 'What do you think, Mrs Stewart?'

'Clear as crystal, blue as the sky. Perfect!' she replied.

'Thank goodness,' Mandy said. 'What with the lamp oil and the smoke from the fire, it's a wonder she's presentable at all!'

'She's more than presentable,' Mrs Stewart

declared, planting a kiss on Ming's smooth head. 'She looks a champion to me!'

Ming yawned as though tired of all the attention, then rolled over on to her back and stretched. Suddenly, she jumped up and butted her head against Mandy's cheek, purring hard.

'I hope so,' Mandy whispered. 'Oh, I hope so.'

Ming travelled to the show in a small wire basket padded with a blue blanket. She protested loudly all the way there, sitting on the back seat of the Land-rover between James and Mandy.

'What a fuss!' Mr Hope grumbled, winking at Mandy in the rear-view mirror. 'Don't look so concerned, love,' he added. 'All cats make a terrible racket in vehicles.'

'She's fine, Mandy,' her mother assured her. 'She's just unused to the motion.'

The journey to the agricultural centre was a short one and soon they were pulling into a parking area already jam-packed with cars, trucks and trailers. A huge yellow banner flapped in a cooling breeze from the top of the massive building, proclaiming this the 'Governing Council of the Cat Fancy Show'.

'Phew!' said James. 'How many people own cats on this island?'

'People travel far and wide to get to shows like this one,' Mrs Hope explained. 'This is a shop window for breeders, plus it gives them a chance to see how their own cats match up to the animals of fellow breeders.'

'It's also a fun day out for cat owners who just want to enjoy their cats,' said Adam Hope.

Mandy lifted Ming out of the car. The basket was quite heavy, but she tried not to swing the Siamese about as she walked along. Inside the vast hall, Emily Hope shook hands with several of the organisers and introduced Mandy, Ming and James. Then she took her place behind a long plastic-topped table and began to set out the instruments she would need for vetting in the cats.

Mandy joined a line of people waiting with their animals to see the vet. Each cat had to pass a simple veterinary inspection before it was allowed to take part in the show. The noise in the hall was deafening, the buzz of voices competing with the meows of what seemed like a thousand or more cats! James put his hands over his ears, but Ming, Mandy noticed, didn't seem to mind. She was quite content now that she was out of the car, and sat on her blanket looking around with great curiosity. Mandy put her ear to the basket and heard Ming purring away happily to herself.

All around the hall, banners announced different breed types. Each group had its own judge and Mandy looked around for where she would be taking Ming.

'Adolescents,' she read. 'Maiden, Debutante, Senior. Gosh, where do we go?'

'Over there.' Adam Hope pointed helpfully as he came up behind them. 'See the sign that says Novice? That's you.'

A steward handed Mandy a tag with a number on it and a vetting-in slip. She shuffled along with Ming in the basket until she reached the third vet in the line, an important-looking man in a white coat. As she stopped in front of him, she caught her mother's eye and smiled. The vet took Mandy's form, then lifted Ming out and quickly checked her skin for signs of ringworm. Her nose was dry and clear, her eyes bright.

'She's in peak condition,' he smiled, putting Ming back in the basket. 'Good luck, young lady. Next!'

'Thank you,' Mandy mumbled, suddenly

overwhelmed by nerves. What did she have to do
now? She looked around for her mother, but
Emily Hope was examining a long-haired cat with
a blunt, typically Persian face and didn't see her.

'Look,' James hissed. 'We're being called to the
middle of the room.'

In the centre of the high-roofed, echoing
building, a long row of tables held a series of
identical cages. There were already cats inside
some of them, yowling in frustration. Mandy was
told by a steward to put Ming into a cage on the
end of the line. The number on the wire mesh
matched the one she had on her tag. There was a

bowl of water in the cage, and some bedding.
Mandy knew she would have to leave Ming alone
for the judging, so she put her finger through the
mesh and scratched Ming's head in farewell. Ming
didn't seem comfortable as her new friend turned
to go. She stuck her slender paw through the wire
and tried to catch Mandy's hand as she left.

'I won't be far away,' Mandy whispered. 'Be a
good girl. I love you.'

Mandy and her dad joined James amid a crush
of eager spectators at one side of the hall. Mandy
had to stand on tiptoe to see the judges moving
slowly down the line of cats. Her heart was
pounding so hard it made her dizzy.

'How's it going?'

Mandy spun around to find Craig and Sarah
Jane Gibb beside her.

'Oh, hi! I'm so nervous. Ming's over there on
the table. The judges are coming to her now,'
Mandy told them in a rush.

'I thought you were playing football?' James said
to Craig.

'Game's over,' Craig replied. 'Mrs Gibb gave me
a lift. I wanted to see how Ming got on.'

Mandy smiled at him. 'Thanks.'

'She's going to be perfect,' Mrs Gibb said. Her blonde hair had been twisted up into a French plait, but in the bustle of the hall, it had come loose and her plump cheeks were flushed with heat.

'I hope you didn't bring Noodles,' James grinned at her. 'Imagine that dog in here with all these cats!'

'No, he's at home,' said Mrs Gibb. 'Craig told me that tomorrow is your last day on the island. Noodles is really going to miss you both!'

'Er, I could have a go at walking him, if you like,' Craig offered hesitantly.

Even though she was straining to keep an eye on Ming, Mandy turned and looked at him in surprise.

'Craig!' said Sarah Jane Gibb, clearly surprised. 'Really? *You*?'

'I'll have a go,' Craig repeated. 'I like him. He's funny – and he seems to have taken a shine to me.'

'Well, thank you,' Mrs Gibb said warmly. 'That would be a huge favour.'

'Noodles might be the start of a whole new career, Craig!' Mandy teased.

'Don't worry,' Craig shot back, his eyes twinkling. 'I'm not going to be giving up football practice to clean out animal cages or anything – not like some people I could mention!'

'Shhhh!' James urged them. 'Ming's being taken out of her cage.'

All eyes were on the Siamese as she was carried across to the judges' table. In the bright lighting of the hall, her coat gleamed. Her four dark paws and her round, chocolate-coloured cheeks were a wonderful contrast to her pale body.

'Little ghost of a tiger,' Mandy said under her breath.

On the table, Ming lifted her pretty face to the judge. Just to the left, Mandy noticed that a beautiful silver Wedgehead Siamese was being examined. Could Ming win over this sleek and imperious creature?

Then she saw a large Applehead in the arms of a woman who was beaming with pride as she placed that cat on the table in front of the judges.

Mandy nudged James. 'Look, another Applehead!' she whispered. 'But not nearly as beautiful as Ming.'

'It's good to see another Applehead,' said James, fairly.

Mandy could hardly breathe as a succession of cats was brought from their holding cages and paraded in front of the judges. The Wedgeheads had such a distinctive look, but none of them had the charm of Ming, in Mandy's opinion.

She held her breath while Ming was being carefully examined but it was all over very quickly – and then, a steward picked Ming up and carried her back to her cage.

It seemed to Mandy that hours passed while more cats were brought forward and taken back. The room became a blur of white coats and beautiful animals.

'It doesn't matter,' Mandy said to James, after another Applehead had made an appearance. Clearly, they had a loyal following on the island. Mandy wondered briefly if they were all related to Gateau! 'It really doesn't matter if she doesn't win a prize. After all ...'

James put a finger to his lips to shush her. His eyes were riveted on the judges as, at last, a metallic announcement rang out from a Tannoy system that echoed around the building.

'In the Oriental category, Novice class . . .'

'This is it!' Sarah Jane Gibbs whispered, clutching at Mandy's sleeve. Mandy looked over to where her mother was standing and waved. Adam Hope slipped an arm around Mandy's shoulders. He was straining forward, frowning in concentration.

'Best of breed award goes to . . .'

Mandy squeezed her eyes shut.

'Sud Su Ming, an eighteen-month-old Applehead owned by Mr Thomas Allardyce of Beaumont, Jersey.'

Mandy felt her heart do a somersault as applause erupted around the room. Adam Hope let out a whoop of triumph and Mandy's mum came hurrying over. Mandy was enveloped in hugs from all sides.

'Congratulations! Well done! You worked so hard!'

'Thomas will be thrilled!'

'So will Mrs Stewart!'

'Thank you,' Mandy said, wondering how quickly she would be able to see Ming. She edged forward, trying to get a glimpse of the Siamese. Suddenly, the crowd began to stream forward to gather up their animals and Mrs Hope eased Mandy along into the middle of the room.

Ming was sitting in her cage on the table, gazing about her in fascination. A bright-red rosette and gold medallion had been pinned to one side and a red winner's certificate was attached to the wire, fluttering temptingly in the breeze from the overhead fans. Ming put out a paw and tried to catch it through the mesh.

'Ming!' Mandy said, opening the lid and reaching in to pick her up. The Siamese greeted her noisily, making a kind of mewling and rumbling sound, as Mandy kissed her face. Ming put her two soft front paws on Mandy's cheeks and touched her nose to Mandy's chin.

'You won,' she told Ming. 'You won for the Appleheads! You beat the Wedgeheads!'

Ming didn't seem interested. Instead she took a swipe at the glinting gold medallion and sent it clattering to the floor.

Mandy laughed and hugged the beautiful cat tighter as people began to gather around: Craig and Sarah Jane Gibb, Jennifer and James, all smiling and reaching out to pet the adorable little Siamese. Mandy was thrilled that Ming had won, but all the medallions and rosettes in the world were not as important to her as the friends she'd made in Beaumont – people as well as animals!

*Look out for more Animal Ark 2-books-in-1
special editions . . .*

PUPPIES IN A PUZZLE

LABRADOR ON THE LAWN: Mandy and James
are staying with her parents at a holiday cottage in
the Lake District when they spot a mischievous
Labrador on their lawn. James's dog Blackie is
delighted to have found a friend, but with no
identification or collar, how will the Hopes find
her owner? And why does she seem so at home in
the cottage?

DALMATIAN IN THE DALES: On their way to
investigate deer poachers operating nearby,
Mandy and James discover a confused and footsore
Dalmatian named Echo. Now it isn't just the
deer that are in trouble. Can Mandy help Echo's
owners to work out why their dog has suddenly
started running away?

Look out for more Animal Ark 2-books-in-1 Special editions . . .

PUPPIES IN PERIL

PUP AT THE PALACE: On a visit to Buckingham Palace, Mandy spots a Labrador puppy, and then sees him again all over London. Who does the puppy belong to?

DOG AT THE DOOR: Mandy finds a pregnant Golden Retriever tied up outside Animal Ark, but no sign of her owner. Who could be responsible?

Look out for more Animal Ark 2-books-in-1 Special editions . . .

KITTENS IN TROUBLE

KITTENS IN THE KITCHEN: Mr Williams, the caretaker at Mandy's school, is furious when a stray cat has a litter in his kitchen. He wants the kittens and their mum out of his house as soon as possible. Will Mandy be able to find owners for them all in just one week?

KITTENS IN THE COLD: Mandy and James are helping to raise money for sick little Alex Hasting's treatment. Alex's pet kitten, Amber, is helping keep her spirits up, but when Amber vanishes, Alex is heartbroken. Where could the kitten be?